She shrugged. "W[...]
to town after a[...]
bound to talk."

"No doubt," Luke ad[...]

"All good stuff," she to[...]

He lifted his mug, swallowed a mouthful of coffee.
"It seems that you have me at a disadvantage."

"How so?"

"You obviously know my name—and apparently a lot
more—but I don't know yours."

She touched a hand to the bib of her apron.
"Oh. I forgot my name tag today," she realized.
"Eva Rose Armstrong."

He set down his mug and proffered his hand.
"It's a pleasure to meet you, Eva Rose Armstrong."

She felt a tingle through her veins as her palm slid
against his. His hand was wide and strong, with
calluses that attested to a familiarity with manual
labor. It was a man's hand, and every womanly part
of her responded to the contact.

"Eva," she said. "My friends call me Eva."

"Are we going to be friends, Eva?"

"I think so," she said, not daring to admit that she
already hoped "friends" was only the beginning of
what they would be to one another.

"I could probably use a friend," he admitted, releasing
her hand to pick up his fork again. "I don't think I
have any left in this town."

MONTANA MAVERICKS:
THE GREAT FAMILY ROUNDUP—
Real cowboys and real love in Rust Creek Falls!

Dear Reader,

It's always fun to visit Rust Creek Falls—especially during the festive season!

Not that ranch hand Luke Stockton planned to go home for the holidays. In fact, for the past dozen years, he hasn't been home at all. But this year, an invitation from his sister has him making an early-December journey from Wyoming to Montana.

Local baker Eva Armstrong doesn't have the greatest track record with men. And maybe having her heart stomped on time and again should have taught her to be wary, but there isn't anything she wants more than to fall in love, get married, fill her home with babies and her kitchen with the sweet scents of baking.

When Luke sees Eva behind the counter at Daisy's Donut Shop, the attraction is both immediate and mutual. But Luke isn't planning to stay in Rust Creek Falls past the holidays, and he won't let anyone persuade him to change those plans—not even a woman whose kisses are sweeter than buttercream frosting.

But Christmas is a season of miracles, and Eva has faith that Luke will decide to stay in Rust Creek Falls—and with her—not just through the holidays, but forever.

I hope you enjoy Luke and Eva's story and have a wonderful holiday season!

Brenda Harlen

The Maverick's Midnight Proposal

—

Brenda Harlen

Special thanks and acknowledgment are given to Brenda Harlen for her contribution to the Montana Mavericks: The Great Family Roundup continuity.

Recycling programs
for this product may
not exist in your area.

ISBN-13: 978-0-373-62387-7

The Maverick's Midnight Proposal

Copyright © 2017 by Harlequin Books S.A.

Printed in U.S.A.

Brenda Harlen is a former attorney who once had the privilege of appearing before the Supreme Court of Canada. The practice of law taught her a lot about the world and reinforced her determination to become a writer—because in fiction, she could promise a happy ending! Now she is an award-winning, national bestselling author of more than thirty titles for Harlequin. You can keep up-to-date with Brenda on Facebook and Twitter or through her website, brendaharlen.com.

Books by Brenda Harlen

Harlequin Special Edition

Those Engaging Garretts!

The Last Single Garrett
Baby Talk & Wedding Bells
Building the Perfect Daddy
Two Doctors & a Baby
The Bachelor Takes a Bride
A Forever Kind of Family
The Daddy Wish
A Wife for One Year
The Single Dad's Second Chance
A Very Special Delivery
His Long-Lost Family
From Neighbors...to Newlyweds?

Montana Mavericks: The Baby Bonanza

The More Mavericks, The Merrier!

Montana Mavericks:
What Happened at the Wedding?

Merry Christmas, Baby Maverick!

Visit the Author Profile page
at Harlequin.com for more titles.

For my parents,
who exemplify the joys and blessings of home—
not just at the holidays but always.

Prologue

Lee Stanton paused as he entered the room, his gaze caught by the blinking light on his phone indicating that he had a message. He picked it up to check the call history. The same number had shown up on his display more than a dozen times in the past four days, though the caller, who'd identified himself as David Bradford, had only left two messages previously. This would be the third.

He pressed the button to connect to voice mail, then punched in his access code.

"This is David Bradford again, the private investigator from Tulsa, hired by Hudson Jones to track down Luke Stockton from Rust Creek Falls, Montana. Please call me back at 539-555-6234."

Lee hit the erase button.

The investigator was nothing if not persistent, and the client—Hudson Jones—was obviously getting his money's worth. Unfortunately, his perseverance wasn't going to pay off this time, because it wasn't possible to find someone who didn't exist, and Luke Stockton had disappeared twelve years earlier on his way to Cheyenne, Wyoming.

Lee tried to put the call out of his mind as he rummaged through the refrigerator, looking for something—anything—to throw together for dinner. After seven hours on horseback feeding cattle and checking perimeter fence, he was cold and tired and hungry. And apparently long overdue for a trip to the grocery store.

He pulled a bottle of beer out of the fridge and twisted off the cap. He tipped the bottle to his lips as he picked up the phone again, dialing from memory the number for Peppe's Pizza.

While he waited for his dinner to be delivered, he turned on the television and flipped through the twelve channels that were included with basic cable as part of his rent. But nothing on the screen held his attention for long.

For the past dozen years, he'd walked the right side of the law, working from sunup to sundown, falling into bed exhausted at the end of the day. But no matter how fatigued his body was, he couldn't escape the memories that continued to haunt his dreams. Memories of a past he'd wanted only to leave behind. Now he couldn't help but wonder if that past had caught up with him.

...hired by Hudson Jones to track down Luke Stockton...

He opened the laptop he'd picked up secondhand and kept plugged in because the battery didn't hold much of a charge. He opened a browser, then started a search for Hudson Jones.

The results were numerous and instantaneous, and a quick skim of the headlines revealed that Hudson Jones was a millionaire cowboy originally from Oklahoma. Since he knew that Luke Stockton had never been to Oklahoma and hadn't rubbed elbows with any millionaires in his past, he figured the PI had taken a wrong turn somewhere. He was about to close the browser when a headline announcing Hudson Jones's marriage caught his eye. The name of the man's wife: Bella Stockton.

Bella? Married?

Stunned, he clicked on the link and found himself looking at a photo of the millionaire cowboy and his beautiful bride. The caption indicated that the couple had exchanged vows early in June—almost six months earlier.

Lee's heart hammered against his ribs as he leaned toward the screen for a closer look. The stunning young woman in the white gown didn't bear much resemblance to the awkward teen he remembered. Except for the eyes. Even in an online photograph, even after so much time had passed, there was no mistaking those big brown eyes.

He blinked away the moisture that blurred his vision and finally acknowledged the truth that was staring back at him: Hudson Jones's bride was indeed Luke's little sister.

And if her new husband had hired a PI to find Luke, then Bella must have told him about losing touch with her siblings. Maybe she'd even asked Hudson to help her find them.

Lee shook his head and tipped the bottle to his mouth again. He was only speculating about her thoughts and motives. He had no way of knowing if Bella wanted to find Luke, but the possibility tugged at him.

Half an hour later, after he'd finished another beer and half of his pizza, he finally picked up the phone and dialed the PI's number.

Chapter One

Anticipation and trepidation wore on Luke with every mile on his tires throughout the drive to Rust Creek Falls. The scenery outside his window was a blur as memories of his first twenty-one years played through his mind like an old movie—and not one with a happy ending.

He'd traveled from Cheyenne to Butte the day before and crashed in a cheap motel. Though his body had craved sleep, his mind wouldn't let him rest and he'd stared at the ceiling for a long time, questioning the impulse that had brought him on this journey.

When he woke in the morning, his first thought had been to turn around and go back to Wyoming.

Because he was a coward.

But apparently the fierceness with which he missed his family was stronger than his cowardice, because instead of turning back, he pushed forward.

After fueling himself with an extra large coffee, he'd started back on the road to Rust Creek Falls. Three and a half hours later, he was almost there.

His gaze searched for the familiar sign that welcomed visitors to town. Twelve years earlier the sign had been old and worn, so it was possible that the marker was no longer standing or—if it was—it might be faded so much that the paint was impossible to read. It didn't matter. Luke didn't need a marker to let him know he'd arrived. Even if he hadn't recognized the terrain, he would have known it in his gut.

But twelve years was a long time, and people changed more quickly than the towns they lived in. Bella hadn't even been a teenager when he left; now she was a woman—and a wife.

Mrs. Bella Jones.

He shook his head, still unable to believe that his little sister was all grown up, still struggling to come to terms with the time he'd lost with his family. And the staggering weight of guilt, because he knew it was his fault.

Of course, Bella didn't know that. Because if she did, she would never have made the effort to find him. More likely, she would have been grateful that he'd left town, and happy he'd stayed away. But she deserved to know the truth—all of his brothers and sisters deserved the truth. A truth that Luke had been too ashamed to tell them, and the grief and remorse weighed on him still.

Although a dozen years had passed since he left Montana, in all that time, he'd never forgotten—or stopped missing—the family he used to have. Since he left Rust Creek Falls, not a single day passed without him thinking about the family he'd walked away from. Bailey and Daniel had gone with him, and the three oldest brothers had stuck close together—at least for a while.

Over the years, he'd lost count of the number of times he'd thought about going home—only to remember all the reasons he'd left. For Luke, "you can't go home again" was more than a catchphrase—it was the reality of his life.

So why was he trying to change that reality now?

Because Bella wanted to see him.

He'd finally called her from the motel the night before to tell her that he was on his way. Partly because he was desperate to hear her voice and partly because he knew that if she was expecting him, he'd be less inclined to turn around and head back to Wyoming.

He'd let her down once, but he wouldn't do it again.

Now he was finally going home—a prospect that filled him with anticipation and more than a little bit of trepidation. As a result of one foolish, youthful error in judgment, he'd lost them all: his parents—Rob and Lauren, and his six siblings—Bailey, Danny, Jamie, Bella, Dana and Liza.

His error.

He tried to push the painful memories aside, because he knew that there was no way to go back in time and do things differently. But sometimes, late at night and deep in dreams, he allowed himself to make a different choice. A smarter choice. And in those dreams, he woke up in the same house he'd lived in for the first twenty-one years of his life, his mother making breakfast in the kitchen while he crawled out of bed, grumbling about the early hour as he dressed in the dark and headed out to the barn to help his father and brothers with the chores.

And every time he dreamed about them, he awakened with such a huge, heavy weight on his chest, he wondered how it was possible that his broken heart was still beating. Then he'd grab a granola bar or pour himself a bowl of cereal and head out to the barn at whatever ranch he was currently working and throw himself into the physical labor, as if successfully wrestling bales of hay would somehow help him overcome the grief and guilt.

His foot eased off the accelerator as he approached the town limits, doubts again battering at him from all directions. Was he really going to do this? Was he, finally, after so many years, going to see his sisters and brothers again?

He'd programmed his GPS to take him to Just Us Kids—the day care facility owned by Hudson Jones's family and where Bella was employed as a manager. The day care hadn't existed twelve years ago, which made him wonder how many other businesses had come and gone in that period of time. Was Crawford's General Store still the only place in town to buy a quart of milk? Did the Ace in the Hole still have the flickering neon sign that beckoned local cowboys with the promise of cold beer and pretty girls? Was the coffee at Daisy's Donut Shop still always hot and fresh?

He could use some of that coffee now. Especially when he glanced at the display on his GPS and saw that his ETA was less than fifteen minutes.

Less than fifteen minutes after more than twelve years.

His fingers tightened on the steering wheel as he drove down Cedar Street, the winter finery on display reminding him that Christmas was less than three weeks away. Garlands and twinkling lights festooned all the storefronts, and a dusting of fresh snow on the sidewalks added to the holiday atmosphere.

Even in Wyoming, he'd heard about the flood that had devastated Rust Creek Falls a few years back, but the community had obviously come together to rebuild.

He'd expected—maybe even hoped—that the town had changed, but everything looked very much the same.

He impulsively turned the corner toward Daisy's Donut Shop, desperate not just for a quick cup of coffee but also a few extra minutes to regain control of his emotions before facing his sister.

He pushed the door open and joined the line at the counter. An elderly man, headed to a table with a mug of steaming coffee in his hand, nodded in his direction.

Just a friendly resident greeting a stranger in town—or so Luke believed until the man said, "Nice to see you, Luke."

The gruff voice was as familiar as Old Gene's face. "Good morning, Mr. Strickland."

"You home for the holidays?" the old man asked.

Home.

The word tugged at something inside him.

Was this his home? He'd been wandering for so long, never setting down roots in any one place, that the word was almost unfamiliar to him.

Unfamiliar and yet oh-so-inviting.

"Just here to visit my sister," he said.

Gene nodded. "She'll be glad to see you."

Luke hoped he was right.

The old man carried his coffee to a booth, where a group of his contemporaries was already seated and waiting for him.

A middle-aged man with graying hair and a much younger blonde woman stepped up to the counter next to place their order. Luke recognized the man as Ben Dalton—the only attorney in town. Ben spotted Luke when he turned to speak to his companion and his eyes widened in obvious surprise. After shaking Luke's hand, Ben introduced his female companion.

"This is my law partner, Maggie Crawford." Ben winked. "I stole her away from a big firm in Los Angeles."

"Then you're a long way from home," Luke said to the woman.

She shook her head. "This is my home now."

"Maggie's married to Jesse Crawford," Ben told him.

"Jesse went to school with my brother Bailey," Luke explained the connection to Maggie. And he'd gone to school with Ben's daughter, Paige.

"Small world," she murmured.

"So it would seem," Luke agreed. "Although Rust Creek Falls has grown even more than I realized if it's able to support two lawyers now."

"Four," Ben corrected. "My daughter, Lindsay, has been working with us since she passed the bar last year. And Maggie's brother, Ryan Roarke, hung up a shingle after he married Kristen Dalton."

"Good to know there are options if I find myself in need of legal services," Luke said.

"Speaking of legal services," Maggie said. "We've got to get to Kalispell for a settlement conference."

Ben nodded. "It was good to see you again, Luke."

"You, too," Luke said. "And nice to meet you, Maggie."

As the two attorneys turned and walked away, he stepped up to the counter.

"Can I help you?"

He glanced from the tempting variety of sweets in the glass-fronted display case to the even more tempting woman behind the counter, and awareness hummed in his veins. Or maybe he'd just imagined the sensation. Maybe what he'd felt was simply relief that here, finally, was someone who didn't know him or his history. Because the gorgeous blonde with wide blue eyes wasn't anyone from his past. If he'd met her before, he was certain he would have remembered.

She followed up the question with a smile, drawing his gaze to the curve of her glossy pink lips. Yeah, her mouth looked a lot sweeter than the glazed donuts for sale, but he'd come back to Rust Creek Falls for one reason and it wasn't to enjoy the local sights—no matter how pretty they might be.

"Coffee," he suddenly remembered. "Large. Black."

Those beautiful blue eyes sparkled with humor. "For here or to go?"

"To go."

She selected a tall paper cup, filled it from the pot then snapped on a lid.

"Thanks." He passed her his money in exchange for the beverage.

She smiled at him again. "You're welcome."

"Large café mocha with extra whipped cream."

Eva Armstrong regretfully shifted her attention from the backside of the handsome cowboy making his way to the door to her next customer. Ellie Traub was a regular who always ordered an old-fashioned glazed along with her large mocha and carried both to a table where she'd sit with Mary and Rita Dalton—sisters-in-law by marriage—and chat about all the comings and goings in town.

"That Luke Stockton sure grew up to be a handsome man," Ellie commented.

Eva mentally assigned the name to the cowboy, satisfied that it fit—even if it didn't answer any of the questions racing through her brain.

"Of course, they were all good-looking boys," Ellie continued.

"Who?" Eva asked.

"Luke, Bailey and Daniel. And Jamie, too, of course." She used the tongs to select a donut from the case and set it on a plate. "I didn't remember that Jamie had so many brothers."

The older woman nodded. "Rob and Lauren had seven kids altogether—four boys and three girls."

Eva punched the order into the cash register.

"And then, when they died in that accident..." Ellie let the words trail off as she shook her head. "Of course, you were probably too young to remember that. It was close to a dozen years ago now."

Twelve years meant that Eva would have been thirteen when they died. And now that she had the reference of a timeline, she did vaguely recall hearing about a car accident that resulted in the deaths of a local rancher and his wife and orphaned their children. In fact, one of the daughters, Bella, had been a year behind Eva in school.

She handed the customer's change across the counter. "Have a good day, Mrs. Traub."

"Thanks," Ellie said, and carried her mug and plate away from the counter.

Eva turned with a smile to the next customer in line but was admittedly distracted by thoughts of Luke Stockton. In fact, she felt a little dazed after the brief encounter with the handsome cowboy, as if she'd been hit over the head with a sack of flour.

Of course, she had a habit of falling hard and fast—

and always for the wrong men. But no matter how many times her heart ended up bruised, she refused to give up hope. Just like the fairy-tale princess who believed that someday her prince would come, Eva believed that her soul mate was out there somewhere.

Or maybe, just maybe, he was right here in Rust Creek Falls now.

The rest of the morning passed in a blur. The donut shop did a brisk business, which kept her hands busy but didn't prevent her mind from speculating about the new man in town.

"You trying to rub the Formica right off that table?" asked a voice behind her.

Eva glanced back at Tracie, the cook who worked the lunch shift. "I guess my mind was wandering," she admitted as she dropped the cloth onto the tray filled with plates and cups that she'd already cleared away.

"Maybe it could wander back to the kitchen and get started making a lemon meringue pie."

"I thought apple and coconut were on the menu today."

Tracie nodded. "But I got a call-in order for a lemon meringue." She looked at the slip where she'd written the customer's name and number. "Lydia Grant. She's making dinner for her fiancé tonight and apparently lemon meringue pie is his favorite."

Eva knew that, of course. Because Lydia's fiancé was Zach Dalton, a rancher who had recently moved to Rust Creek Falls with his father and siblings after the devastating loss of his mother in a house fire.

Unlike so many men, Zach was a traditional kind of guy who wanted to get married and have children. In fact, he was so determined that he'd even advertised in the *Gazette* for a woman who was an excellent cook and homemaker and loved kids, dogs and horses.

Eva had gone on a few dates with Zach before he'd fallen in love with Lydia—who didn't have any of the traits that he'd claimed to be looking for in a wife. Now Eva, who had fulfilled all of his requirements—at least on paper—was being enlisted to make Zach's favorite pie for his future wife to serve to him.

As she carried the tray of dirty dishes to the kitchen, she acknowledged that this was only the most recent in a string of romantic disappointments.

But her heart wasn't heavy as she began to measure the ingredients for the pastry. Because she wasn't thinking about Zach and Lydia's engagement—she was thinking about the return to Rust Creek Falls of sexy cowboy Luke Stockton.

Luke sat in his truck in the parking lot outside Just Us Kids Day Care Center. Somewhere inside the brick building with the colorful sign that looked as if it had been written in thick crayon by a first grader, his sister was waiting for him. He took another minute to finish his coffee as he continued to sit and stare at the double doors that would take him from the present to his past.

He lifted the cup to his lips and let his gaze shift to the fenced-in play area where a group of kids, bundled up in thick snowsuits, hats, mittens and boots, were playing in the deep snow. Despite the frigid temperatures, they were laughing and giggling and having a great time. He didn't know how old they were—three? four?—but watching them reminded him of Bella when she'd been a similar age.

As a child, she'd had seemingly endless energy and

enthusiasm, and she'd found joy in every aspect of life. Of course, that was a lot of years before their parents were killed, sucking all the joy out of all their lives.

Before he could go too far down that dark path, he stepped out of the truck and made his way toward the entrance. He lifted his arm to reach for the handle, then hesitated again. Over the past dozen years, he'd never let himself think about a potential reunion with his siblings because he never believed he would come back to Rust Creek Falls. Now that the moment was here, he was paralyzed by his own doubts and fears.

Apparently his sister felt differently, because the door he was staring at suddenly flung open.

"You're here!"

Those two words were the only warning Luke got before Bella launched herself into his arms. He caught her—a reflex action—and she pressed her cheek to his, covering his face with kisses and tears.

The unexpected outpouring of affection made his heart swell inside his chest, so much that his ribs actually ached.

"You're really here," she said again.

"I'm *really* here," he confirmed.

"I know you said you were coming," she acknowledged, "but I've been waiting for so long that it feels like forever."

His arms tightened around her. It felt like forever to him, too. And though he'd had more than a few reservations about returning to Rust Creek Falls, right now, with Bella in his arms, he was certain that he'd made the right decision.

All too soon, she was drawing away again. "Come on," she said, tugging on his arm. "I want you to meet my husband." Her eyes sparkled as her lips curved. "We've been married for almost six months, and I still get such a thrill every time I say that."

"I feel a shock to hear you say it," Luke confessed. But he was eager to meet Hudson Jones—and to thank him for hiring the PI who had tracked him down.

When he stepped into the building, he was immediately enveloped by warmth—a welcome reprieve from the bitter winds blowing outside—and assailed by various sounds and scents: crying and cooing and singing; baby powder and Play-Doh and fresh gingerbread.

"We're baking cookies for the toddlers to decorate today," she explained. "And to eat, during snack time."

"I guess day care isn't all about story time and building blocks," he mused.

She laughed. "You have no idea."

He took a minute to catch his breath and survey the space. The tiles beneath his boots were multicolored, the walls were painted sunshine yellow and decorated with artwork that he suspected had been done by children who attended the day care. "How did you end up working here?"

"The facility was opening at a time when I was desperate for a job," she admitted. "Jamie's wife died after giving birth to their three babies, so I came home from college to help him with Henry, Jared and Katie."

He'd thought nothing could surprise him more than discovering that Bella was married, and now she was telling him that his youngest brother had also married—and been widowed—and was a father. "Triplets?"

She nodded.

"And you left school to be his babysitter?"

"He's family," she said simply, as if that explained

everything. "And the only brother I had left after you, Bailey and Danny took off."

"Bella—"

"We'll talk about that later," she interjected, hooking one arm through Luke's and raising her other hand to knock on a partially open door beside the main reception desk.

"Come in."

She pushed the door open the rest of the way. "Hudson, there's someone here that I want you to meet."

The man behind the desk slid his chair back and stood up. The smile that lit his eyes when he looked at his wife assured Luke that he was just as much in love with Bella as she obviously was with him.

Then his gaze shifted, and cooled noticeably. "You must be Luke."

He nodded and shook the proffered hand. "It's nice to meet the man who won my sister's heart."

"She won mine first," Hudson said. "And I'd do anything for my beautiful bride, so I was pleased to hear that David Bradford was successful in tracking you down in Wyoming."

"I'm grateful for your efforts," Luke said sincerely.

"I just want Bella to be happy," Hudson said.

Luke understood what the man was saying—and what he wasn't. Hudson had hired the private investigator to find Bella's siblings because it was what she wanted, but he wouldn't tolerate anyone—even her family—hurting his wife. Although Hudson's demeanor made him a little wary, Luke couldn't help but respect his new brother-in-law for wanting to protect his bride.

"I *am* happy," Bella assured him. "And I know this is going to be the best Christmas ever, not just because

it's my first as Mrs. Hudson Jones—" she sent an ador-
ing look toward her husband "—but because Luke is finally home and Danny is planning his Christmas Eve
wedding."

Luke opened his mouth, intending to tell her that he
wouldn't be staying in Rust Creek Falls for Christmas,
but the last part of her statement pushed everything else
from his mind.

"Our Danny?"

Bella nodded.

"He's here—in Rust Creek Falls?"

"You didn't know?"

Luke shook his head. "We kind of lost touch a few
years back," he admitted.

"He's been here since October," Bella told him now.
"After he saw an interview with Jamie on *The Great
Roundup*, he realized he missed his family and finally
decided to come back."

"What's *The Great Roundup*?"

His sister seemed surprised by the question. "Don't
you watch TV?"

"Not a lot," he admitted.

"*The Great Roundup* is a reality show, similar to *The
Amazing Race* but with a Western theme," Hudson explained. "There are various challenges of skill and sur-
vival, and the winner gets a million dollars."

"And you watch this?" Luke asked, his tone dubious.

"Travis Dalton and Brenna O'Reilly are on the show,"
his brother-in-law explained.

"And they're engaged!" Bella exclaimed.

Although Luke didn't know Travis or Brenna, he knew
the Daltons and O'Reillys were longtime residents of
Rust Creek Falls. But he was more interested in what

she'd said about their brother than the details of a reality show. "And you said Danny's engaged, too?"

"To Annie Lattimore," she said, naming their brother's high school sweetheart.

"I should have known," he realized. "Danny never wanted to leave Rust Creek Falls—or Annie."

"Then why did he?" Bella wondered. "Why did *you*?"

He answered with the truth—or at least part of it. "Because we couldn't stay. The grandparents made it clear they didn't want us hanging around, that even four kids were too much of a burden."

"Not long after you left, they sent Dana and Liz away, too," Bella told him.

Hudson slid an arm across her shoulders—a wordless gesture of support and comfort—while Luke just looked on helplessly.

"I'm so sorry," he told her. "We—*I*—honestly thought it was the best decision at the time."

"Well, you're here now," she said again, blinking away the tears that had filled her eyes. "And Dana's been found, too—she lives with her adoptive family in Portland—so I'm confident that we'll all be together again soon."

Luke shifted his gaze to his brother-in-law. "Has your PI succeeded in tracking down everyone else?"

"Not yet," Hudson admitted. "But he's got some leads and I'm sure we'll see results soon." He glanced down as his cell phone buzzed. "Sorry—that's a business call I need to take."

"Of course," Bella acknowledged, nudging Luke back toward the door, then closing it softly after she'd followed him out. "I need to get back to work, too," she said apologetically.

Luke nodded. "Maybe we can catch up some more later."

"We'll definitely catch up later," she immediately responded. "But now you're probably exhausted after your long drive, so why don't you go back to our house, put your feet up and relax? Even have a nap if you want."

"A nap?" he echoed.

"Nap time isn't just for preschoolers," she assured him, pressing something into his palm.

He stared at the key, wondering how it was so easy for her to not only accept his sudden reappearance in her life but even open up her home to him after so much time had passed. "I don't want to impose," he told her.

"It's not an imposition," she insisted. "We're happy to have you."

He believed that *she* was happy, but he didn't think her husband was overjoyed.

"You and Hudson are still newlyweds," he protested. "I should get a room at the boarding house so you aren't tripping over me."

She laughed. "Obviously you haven't yet seen the house. When you do, you'll realize that there's plenty of room and no reason to worry about anyone tripping over anyone else."

Still, he wasn't entirely comfortable with the idea of staying with the sister he'd had no contact with for more than a decade. Or maybe it was the prospect of staying in Rust Creek Falls at all that made him uneasy.

"Please," she added, and with that single word, the last of his resistance melted away.

"Okay," he relented. "I'll stay for a couple of days."

"That's a good start," she agreed.

Chapter Two

Luke was smiling and shaking his head as he walked out of the day care and headed back to his truck. He'd forgotten how sneaky his sister could be—and how he'd never been able to refuse anything she asked. But he was grateful for her invitation and looking forward to the opportunity to catch up with her and Jamie and Danny.

He was also curious to check out Bella and Hudson's house, but he wasn't quite ready to put his feet up. What he was, his growling stomach pointed out, was hungry.

Earlier, his gut had been so twisted up in knots over the impending reunion with his sister that he hadn't been able to eat anything. Now that the initial meeting was over, he realized he was famished.

He hadn't forgotten about the Ace in the Hole—or the thick, juicy burgers that were served with a mountain of crispy fries. In fact, the memory alone was enough to make his mouth water and, when his stomach rumbled again, he steered his truck toward Sawmill Street.

But for reasons he couldn't fathom, he abruptly turned off Sawmill onto North Broomtail and pulled up in front of Daisy's Donut Shop again.

* * *

After graduating from high school, Eva had wanted to follow her passion and pursue a diploma in baking and pastry arts. But following her heart had led to heartache more times than she could count, so she'd listened to the urging of her parents and opted to study accounting instead. She'd just completed her first year when her father was diagnosed with lymphoma, so she'd returned to Rust Creek Falls to support her family and postponed the rest of her studies.

She'd been fortunate to get a job at Daisy's Donut Shop. The part-time hours had allowed her to earn a little bit of income while also providing the flexibility she'd needed to take her father to his various doctors' appointments and therapies. When Ray Armstrong had finished his treatments, she'd been able to increase her hours and now she was working full-time. Since the doctors had officially declared her dad to be in remission, he'd been pressuring his daughter to return to school and complete her degree. In the spirit of compromise, she'd been taking some online courses and was now only a few courses shy of completion, but she was still happier baking than studying.

Her friends liked to tease that she would be the perfect wife and homemaker, but she hadn't yet met a man who agreed with their assessment.

Maybe having her heart stomped on time and time again should have taught her to be wary, but there wasn't anything she wanted more than to fall in love, get married, fill her home with babies and her kitchen with the sweet scents of baking, so she was trusting fate to put the right man in her path.

In the meantime, she kept busy filling Daisy's display case with mouthwatering goodies. Since the morning rush had passed and it was still early for lunch, Eva took advantage of the lull to brew a fresh pot of coffee, then sipped a cup while she took inventory of the goodies that remained. The white chocolate cranberry cookies had sold out, which made her feel pretty good. Her boss had protested that there was no need to expand their offerings beyond the tried-and-true muffins and donuts, but Eva had been playing around with some of her grandmother's recipes, tweaking here and there, and the residents of Rust Creek Falls—most of them creatures of habit—had overcome their reluctance and started to look forward to daily specials.

Today's pumpkin spice muffins had been gone within the first two hours of the shop's opening, the sticky buns had sold out shortly after and there were only two eggnog biscotti remaining in the jar on the counter. She pulled an empty tray out of the case—the cheesecake-stuffed snickerdoodles had also been decimated by the morning crowd—replaced the liner and set out neatly decorated gingerbread boy and girl cookies.

She glanced up when the bell over the door chimed, and her heart immediately skipped a beat.

He was back.

The handsome cowboy with the sexy voice and troubled eyes.

She'd hoped to see him again, but she hadn't expected that her wish would come true so quickly.

"You're back," she said, because her brain couldn't seem to focus on anything else.

He seemed surprised that she'd remembered him from earlier—or maybe he thought he should remember her from years ago—but he only said, "I'm hungry."

"Then you've come to the right place." She smiled, wanting him to feel welcome, and wishing she could ease the tension that was evident in the line of his jaw and the set of his shoulders. "Breakfast or lunch hungry?"

"Huh?" He looked at her blankly.

She didn't know where he'd gone after he'd left the donut shop earlier, but it was apparent that his mind wasn't occupying the same physical space as his body.

"Are you hungry for breakfast or lunch?" she asked again.

"I don't even know what time it is," he admitted, glancing at the watch on his wrist.

"It's definitely time to get you some food," she decided. "How does a roast beef sandwich with steak-cut fries sound?"

"Delicious."

She smiled again as she filled a mug with coffee and set it on the counter, then gestured to the chair. "Sit."

He sat, then lifted his eyes to meet her gaze. "Are you always this bossy?"

She winked at him. "Only when the occasion warrants."

She left him with his coffee while she slipped into the kitchen to get his food, pausing first to pull out her lip gloss and quickly swipe the wand over her lips.

"He's back," she told Tracie, tucking the tube into her pocket again.

"Who's back?" the cook asked.

"Luke Stockton."

"That's old news," Tracie said, continuing to chop cabbage for the coleslaw she was making. "Half the town saw him in here this morning."

"I don't mean he's back in town," Eva told her, piling

thinly sliced beef onto bread to make his sandwich. "I mean he's back *here*. Sitting at the counter."

"Is that why you're loading up that plate?"

"He said he's hungry."

The cook chuckled. "And the way to a man's heart is through his stomach," she agreed.

Eva felt her cheeks flush. "I'm not interested in his heart."

"Just his body?" Tracie teased. "Can't blame you for that—the man is spectacularly well built."

Eva's cheeks burned hotter. He certainly was that, but that wasn't why she wanted to feed him. Or not entirely.

"He looks a little…lost," she said, adding fries to the plate.

"He hasn't been home to Rust Creek Falls in twelve years," the cook reminded her. "He's probably feeling a little lost."

Twelve years.

Eva couldn't imagine being apart from her family and friends for more than a decade. Even the few months that had passed between visits when she was in college had seemed like an eternity. "I wonder why he stayed away for so long."

"There was a lot of speculation about that," Tracie mused. "But if you want the truth, you'd better ask the man himself."

"I just might do that," she decided.

"Wait," the cook said when she started out of the kitchen.

Eva held back a smile as the other woman added a couple of sprigs of parsley to the plate.

"Presentation matters," Tracie reminded her. "You

know it, or you wouldn't have retouched the gloss on your lips."

Unable to deny that she had done just that, Eva silently took the plate and returned to the counter.

"Thanks," Luke said when she set the meal in front of him.

"Enjoy," she said, and busied herself tidying up the arrangement of mugs as he picked up his fork.

She was glad that he was early for lunch, so that he was the only customer in the donut shop and she was able to focus exclusively on him. Although she suspected that even if she'd had a line all the way to the door, she would have found her attention solely on the handsome stranger.

"Do you want to talk about it?" she asked when he'd polished off the sandwich.

He looked up, obviously surprised by the question, but immediately shook his head.

She gave him another minute before she asked, "Where did you go when you left here this morning?"

He dipped a fry into the ketchup he'd squirted on his plate. "To see my sister."

"I can only imagine how excited Bella must have been when you showed up."

Thick brows drew together over his dark blue eyes. "How'd you know Bella is my sister?" he asked warily.

"I heard Ben Dalton call you Luke," she confided.

"It's quite a jump from my first name to my family connections," he pointed out.

She shrugged. "When someone returns to town after a dozen years, people are bound to talk."

"No doubt," he admitted, his tone grim.

"All good stuff," she told him.

He lifted his mug, swallowed a mouthful of coffee. "It seems that you have me at a disadvantage."

"How so?"

"You obviously know my name—and apparently a lot more—but I don't know yours."

She touched a hand to the bib of her apron. "Oh. I forgot my name tag today," she realized. "Eva Rose Armstrong."

He set down his mug and proffered his hand. "It's a pleasure to meet you, Eva Rose Armstrong."

She felt a tingle through her veins as her palm slid against his. His hand was wide and strong, with calluses that attested to a familiarity with manual labor. It was a man's hand, and every womanly part of her responded to the contact.

"Eva," she said. "My friends call me Eva."

"Are we going to be friends, Eva?" he asked, releasing her hand.

"I think so," she said, not daring to admit that she already hoped *friends* was only the beginning of what they would be to one another.

"I could probably use a friend," he admitted, dredging another fry through ketchup. "I don't think I have any left in this town."

"You haven't stayed in touch with anyone here?"

He shook his head and shoved the fry into his mouth.

"I have to admit that piques my curiosity," she told him.

"You know what they say about curiosity."

She ignored the warning. "Twelve years is a long time to stay away from your family."

"I was working."

The abrupt response and clipped tone cautioned her

to back off, but she pressed on anyway. "You didn't get any time off?"

"Ranching is a full-time job."

She nodded an acknowledgment of the fact. Though her parents both worked in education, no one who lived in Rust Creek Falls was oblivious to the arduous demands of working the land. "No time to make a phone call?"

"How do you know I didn't?" he challenged.

"Did you?"

He pushed his now-empty plate aside. "No."

"Well, you're here now," she said. "That's a start."

"Maybe," he allowed, lifting his mug again, only to discover it was empty.

"More coffee?" Eva offered, wanting to give him an excuse to linger at the counter awhile longer.

Although the lunch crowd would soon fill up the tables, she didn't want to watch Luke Stockton walk out the door because she didn't know when—or even if— she would see him again. And maybe it was unreasonable and irrational, but she couldn't help feeling that the man sitting in front of her was going to change her life—but only if she could get him to stick around long enough to do so.

"No, thanks," he said. "Just the check."

"How about dessert?" she offered as an alternative. "I made the pies fresh this morning, and the coconut cream is a favorite of many customers."

"Actually, I'm more of an apple pie kind of guy."

"We have apple, too."

He rubbed a hand over his flat belly and shook his head. "That sandwich was more than enough to fill the hole in my stomach."

She reluctantly wrote up his check and slid it across the counter.

His fingers brushed hers as he reached for the slip of paper, sending little sparks dancing up her arm and making her wonder how she would respond if he ever really touched her.

Unfortunately, he seemed completely unaffected by the brief contact.

"Thanks," he said. "For the meal and the company."

"My pleasure," she told him.

He retrieved his wallet from the inside pocket of his sheepskin-lined leather jacket, then selected some bills and tucked them under the check before he slid off the stool and rose to his feet.

Her heart sighed as her gaze skimmed over him again. She guessed that he was at least four inches taller than her own five-foot-eight-inch frame, with broad shoulders that tapered to a narrow waist and long legs encased in well-worn denim.

She wanted to tell him that everything was going to be okay, that whatever had caused him to stay away for so long was water under the bridge, that his siblings were all going to welcome him back—because Rust Creek Falls was where he belonged. And she wanted to tell him that she was glad he was home—because she'd been waiting for him her whole life.

But mindful of the brevity of their acquaintance, she wisely kept those thoughts to herself.

Instead, she reached for his check again and impulsively scribbled her cell number on the back of it. "In case you ever need pie...or donuts...or...anything."

Luke looked at the hastily scrawled digits, then at Eva. *Pie...or donuts...or...anything.*
Anything?

Was she hitting on him?

As if she could somehow read the thoughts that circled in his mind, her cheeks flushed, the pink color adding a natural blush to her creamy skin.

Eva Rose Armstrong really was a beautiful woman and maybe, under different circumstances, he might consider what she was offering. Hell, there was no *might* about it. If he'd come to town for any reason other than to reconnect with the family he hadn't seen in a dozen years, he would already have asked when her shift ended and made plans to meet her later.

But he *was* in town to reconnect with his family and he had no time—and even less inclination—for anything else. He'd proven adept enough at messing up his own life; he wasn't going to mess with a pretty young thing who wasn't smart enough to be wary of strangers.

But she'd been kind to him, so he carefully folded the check in half, then tucked it into the inside pocket of his jacket with his wallet. "See ya."

"I hope so," she replied, her lips curving into another sweet smile before he turned away and headed to the exit.

Because that sweet smile seemed to promise all kinds of things that he wasn't sure she meant—and that he couldn't accept even if she did.

Still, as he turned his truck toward Bella and Hudson's house, it was Eva's pretty eyes and warm smile that lingered in his mind.

Luke's first impression of Bella and Hudson's home was that it looked like a million dollars. Of course, his sister's husband was a multimillionaire so it was entirely possible the house they'd purchased from Clive Bickler was worth that much—or more. It was certainly a lot bigger and grander than the home the seven Stockton siblings had shared with their parents, and the newlyweds lived there alone.

He unlocked the door with the spare key, then punched in the code that Bella had given him to disarm the alarm system. A man with Hudson Jones's wealth would want to protect what was his, and Luke appreciated that the protection extended to his sister.

Curious about the house and whatever insights it might give to the couple who lived there, Luke decided to wander around. The home was constructed with high-end materials and included all the latest conveniences, but it wasn't ostentatious. As he made his way from room to room, he couldn't deny that it had a warm and homey feel, and he was pleased to know that his sister had been lucky enough to fall in love with a man who could provide her with all the love and luxuries she deserved.

When he stepped into the family room, his gaze was immediately drawn to the river-rock fireplace and the assortment of photos displayed on the mantel. He crossed the glossy hardwood floor for a closer look. The first picture that caught his eye was of his youngest brother, Jamie, standing next to a woman he thought he recognized as Fallon O'Reilly, with three adorable toddlers at their feet. The next frame contained a wedding photo, and the groom looked enough like Hudson that Luke guessed the man was his brother, but the bride looked vaguely familiar to him, too. Beside that picture was one of Danny, cheek-to-cheek with his high school sweetheart, Annie; beside it was a photo of Dana, all grown-up and proud at her high school graduation.

The smile that tugged at his own lips faded when his gaze shifted to the next photo—an older picture of all the Stockton siblings together with their parents, Rob and Lauren. A reflection of the happy family they'd once been. Before he ruined everything.

Suddenly Luke couldn't bear the thought of facing his sisters and brothers again. He couldn't face the condemnation he was certain he would see in their eyes when they learned the truth about the events of twelve years ago. It would be better for him—for everyone—if he went back to Cheyenne and forgot any ideas about a happy reunion that could never happen.

He retraced his steps to the door, eager to escape the house, the whole town and especially the memories and regrets that assailed him. He yanked his coat off the hanger and was reaching for the door when the sound of the bell stopped him in his tracks.

What was he supposed to do now?

He felt weird answering the door at a house he was only visiting, so he peeked out the window instead.

Almost eight years had passed since he'd last seen his second youngest brother, and his heart gave a hard kick against his ribs when he recognized him on the doorstep now.

He opened the door. "Danny."

"I almost didn't believe Bella when she called to tell me that you were in town," his brother said.

"So you stopped by to see for yourself?"

"Nah, I stopped by because Bella was afraid you might have been spooked by her emotional outburst and decide to take off again before she got home." He looked pointedly at the jacket in Luke's hand. "Was she right?"

"I guess I can't blame her for thinking I'd run...again," he admitted, sliding his jacket back onto the hanger. "There are a lot of memories in this town."

"More good than bad," Danny said.

"The bad are more powerful," he argued.

"Maybe more recent," his brother acknowledged. "Because you've been away for so long."

Danny stepped across the threshold and pulled him in for a man hug. "It's good to see you, Luke."

Luke slapped him on the back as he attempted to swallow the lump in his throat. "You, too, Danny."

His brother cleared his own as he stepped away and moved down the hall toward the kitchen, obviously familiar with the layout of their sister's house. "Bella also said that there were snacks and drinks in the fridge, and to make sure that you didn't go hungry."

"No worries there," Luke said. "I grabbed a bite at Daisy's before I came here."

"Well, I could use some coffee," Danny announced. "You want a cup?"

"Sure." Luke warily eyed the programmable machine that could brew individual cups or full carafes. "If you can figure out how to use that thing."

"It's not as complicated as it looks. The harder task might be finding the coffee."

But it turned out that Bella kept the coffee pods conveniently located in the cupboard directly above the coffee maker. When the coffee was brewed, they took their mugs to the table where Danny told his brother about his reunion with Annie and finally meeting Janie—his daughter.

"And the surprises keep coming," Luke murmured.

"How do you think I felt?" Danny asked. "When I first discovered that Annie had a child, I assumed her husband—ex-husband now—was the father."

"A reasonable assumption," he agreed.

"When we left… I never even considered the possibility that Annie could be pregnant," Danny admitted.

"You were eighteen," Luke reminded him. "Most guys that age are only thinking about sex—not the potential repercussions of it."

"And then I ran away, and I missed the first eleven years of my daughter's life."

Luke stared into his mug. "You didn't run away," he denied. "*I* ran away—and you and Bailey came with me." And the fact that Danny had missed those eleven years with his daughter was one more thing Luke was responsible for. One more wrong he could never make right.

"But now you're home," Danny said, sounding genuinely pleased. As if he'd already forgiven Luke for everything he'd done.

But Danny didn't know the half of it.

Chapter Three

"This isn't my home," Luke said, regretting that it was true. "Not anymore."

"Then why are you here?"

He lifted his cup to his lips as he considered his brother's question. It was the same question he'd asked himself countless times since he'd tossed his duffel bag into his truck and turned it in the direction of Rust Creek Falls.

He still wasn't sure he knew the answer, so he responded with a simple if incomplete truth. "I got a call from Hudson's PI."

"Good to know the guy's finally earned some of the big bucks our brother-in-law is paying him."

"It looks like Hudson has a few bucks to spare," Luke noted, turning his head to encompass the whole room.

"That he does," Danny agreed. "Although it was actually Jamie's wife who started the search last year. Fallon tracked down Dana in Oregon, but she hit a lot of dead ends after that and Hudson offered to take the lead."

It was obvious to both of them that Bella's husband had a lot more resources to throw at the task—and more success as a result.

"Over the years, I'd given a lot of thought to reaching out to our siblings, but I'm not sure I ever would have found the courage to come back if Bradford hadn't made contact."

"We've all been carrying a lot of baggage for a lot of years," Danny noted. "Maybe it's time to let it go and make a fresh start."

It sounded like a good idea to Luke, but he wasn't sure it was possible. "Was it that easy for you?" he asked.

"It wasn't easy at all," his brother said. "But it was necessary."

Luke swallowed another mouthful of coffee.

"So how long are you planning to stay?" Danny asked.

"I haven't thought that far ahead," he admitted.

"There's no specific date that you're expected back in Wyoming?"

He shook his head. "My boss told me to take as much time as I needed."

"Then you can stay for my wedding."

He recalled Bella mentioning plans for a Christmas Eve wedding. "December twenty-fourth is still two-and-a-half weeks away."

"Two-and-a-half weeks isn't a lot of time after so many years," his brother pointed out.

But if he was there for Danny's Christmas Eve wedding, Luke suspected that Bella would insist he stay for Christmas and he wasn't accustomed to celebrating the holidays. In fact, he hadn't celebrated anything in a very long time.

Sensing his hesitation, Danny said, "It would mean a lot to me to have you there."

"Bella and Hudson might not want me hanging around that long," he warned.

"In this house, Bella and Hudson won't even know you're here," Danny said.

"I'll think about it," he decided.

"Or maybe there's another reason you don't want to stay," his brother allowed. "Maybe it's not just cattle and chores waiting for you back in Wyoming."

Luke looked at him blankly.

"Maybe there's a special lady anxiously awaiting your return?" Danny suggested.

He immediately shook his head. "No, there's no one in Wyoming."

But as soon as the words were out of his mouth, an image of the pretty blonde from the donut shop popped into his mind. *Eva.* As pretty and sweet and tempting as the biblical figure for which she was named.

"No one in Wyoming," Danny echoed curiously. "Does that mean there's someone waiting for you somewhere else?"

Luke shook his head again, attempting to shake the image loose. "No," he denied. "There's no one at all."

"That's too bad."

"I like being on my own, with no one to depend on me but me."

"And no one to rely on but you, too," Danny pointed out as he pushed away from the table and went to the refrigerator.

"It works for me," he insisted.

"I thought it worked for me, too, but I was only kidding myself." He pulled out the tray of snacks Bella had prepared and set it in the middle of the table. "I missed a lot of years with Annie and Janie, but I'm determined to make up for that now."

"I'm still trying to get my head around the fact that you're a father—to an eleven-year-old."

"It's been an adjustment for everyone," Danny admitted. "And as much as I want to hate Hank—Annie's ex—because he got to be there when Janie was born, to hold her as a baby, soothe her when she was crying, witness her first steps and take her to school on her first day, I can't. The truth is, I'm grateful that he was there for them, because I wasn't."

"You didn't know," Luke reminded him.

His brother nodded, though he didn't seem reassured by the fact. "Anyway, I can't wait for you to meet her," he said, the pride in his voice unmistakable. "She's smart and funny and absolutely beautiful."

"She must look like her mom, then," Luke teased.

"That she does," Danny agreed. "But the shape of her eyes and the stubborn tilt of her chin are just like our mom."

Luke reached for a cube of cheese.

"Mom and Dad's first grandchild."

His brother nodded. "When I found out that Janie was my daughter, when I got over the shock, I couldn't help but think of Mom and Dad—how they would have responded to the news that they were grandparents."

"They would have been thrilled," he said and popped the cheese into his mouth.

"Yeah," Danny said. "But only after Dad kicked my ass into next week for getting Annie pregnant."

"He would have done exactly that," Bella said from the doorway.

Both Luke and Danny turned. "We didn't hear you come in."

"You were preoccupied with your journey down memory lane—without me," she said, sounding just a little piqued.

"It's a long road," Danny pointed out. "And we only just got started."

"I don't really mind." She settled into the empty chair between them. "I'm just so glad that you're both finally home again."

Luke felt something inside twist painfully. "Rust Creek Falls isn't my home, Bella. Not anymore."

She tipped her chin up and met his gaze squarely. "Of course it is," she insisted. "And after you've spent some time here, you'll realize it's true."

"Bella." He touched a hand to her arm, hoping the contact might ease the harshness of the truth she needed to hear. "I've been living in Wyoming for twelve years— that's my home now."

"But you've never stayed in any one place for more than two years," she pointed out.

He frowned. "How do you know that?"

"It's one of the reasons it took Hudson's PI so long to track you down. The other reason—" she pinned him with a look "—is that Luke Stockton somehow became Lee Stanton."

He picked up a cherry tomato and popped it into his mouth, but his sister wasn't letting him off the hook.

"Why?" she demanded.

Before he could respond, Danny's cell phone buzzed. "That's my cue to run," he said. "Annie went to Kalispell this afternoon for a dress fitting, so I have to pick Janie up from her study group at school."

Luke pushed away from the table and stood up, offering his hand to his brother. Danny shook his hand, then pulled him in for another hug.

"Stop by anytime," he urged his brother. "I know Annie will be happy to see you, and I'm eager for you to meet my daughter."

"I will," Luke promised.

Then Danny gave Bella a quick hug, too, before he disappeared down the hall.

"Now," Bella said, turning her focus back to Luke, "answer my question."

"What question was that?" he hedged, selecting a broccoli spear from the plate.

She snatched it out of his hand before he could lift it to his mouth and held it away from him. "Why were you living in Wyoming as Lee Stanton?"

"It wasn't intentional," Luke told her. "At least, not at first. The bookkeeper at the ranch we were working put me on the payroll as 'Stanton' by mistake and it just seemed like too much effort to try to correct it. When I moved on, I continued to use Stanton so that I could reference my work history under that name. And, in some ways, it was easier to start a new life with a new name."

"But why did you want a new life?" she pressed. "Why did you leave?"

He heard the confusion in her question—and the hurt. "It wasn't an easy decision to make," he admitted, wanting to explain the past and soothe his sister. "But what choice did we have? The ranch was going to be taken by the bank, and the grandparents didn't have room to take us all in—and no interest in doing so. As Gramps said, we were legal adults and they had no obligation to provide us with food or shelter."

Bella's dark brown eyes filled with tears. "I always suspected that they made you leave."

"They didn't make us leave, but they didn't give us

any reason to stay, either. And we thought Jamie, you, Liza and Dana would all be together."

"After they sent Liza and Dana away—" she swiped at a tear that spilled onto her cheek "—there were times I wish they'd sent me and Jamie away, too."

"Was it really so bad?" Luke asked.

"Probably not. We had a roof over our heads and meals on the table. But there was no affection. There was rarely even any warmth or kindness."

"I'm so sorry, Bella."

She shrugged. "It's water under the bridge now. Or mostly, anyway. Because it turns out that you were wrong about the ranch."

"What do you mean?"

"Sunshine Farm doesn't belong to the bank—it belongs to us."

"To you and Hudson?" he guessed, because it seemed a reasonable assumption. Bella's husband obviously had a ton of money, and it was just as obvious he would spend it all to make his wife happy. If the property had been for sale, Luke could imagine Hudson buying it for her without blinking an eye.

But she shook her head. "To you, Bailey, Danny, Jamie, me, Liza and Dana."

He stared at her, uncomprehending. "But…how?"

"When Dad remortgaged the property to fix the barn and buy the new equipment, he also bought mortgage insurance."

Luke was stunned. Even at twenty-one, he'd had a pretty good picture of the tight financial situation at Sunshine Farm. He'd heard his parents talking about it in hushed and worried tones when they thought their children were asleep. He'd recognized the strain in his father's voice, seen it in the lines that furrowed his mother's brow. He'd listened to them argue about the purchase of secondhand equipment that they couldn't afford but desperately needed to keep the ranch operating, and he knew that they'd had to remortgage the property. He hadn't known they'd also arranged for insurance on that mortgage.

He and Bailey and Danny had left because they hadn't believed that there was any other option. For the past twelve years, they'd worked for other people when they could have been working at Sunshine Farm. Or maybe it was naive to think that they might have been able to keep the ranch going—a difficult enough task when Rob Stockton had been around to oversee the operation. More likely, Luke and his brothers would have run the ranch into the ground and been forced to sell anyway.

"We just discovered that the property had been transferred into all of our names, pursuant to the terms of Mom and Dad's will, a few months ago when Zach Dalton approached Jamie to see if we were interested in selling," Bella explained.

"Are you going to sell?" he asked.

"That's a decision we have to make together," she said. "*All* of us."

"I guess that explains why you're so eager for a family reunion," he noted.

"We only found out about the property a few months ago," she said again. "We've been looking for you a lot longer than that." She smiled again. "And now you're finally here."

"Are you sure Hudson doesn't mind me crashing here? Because I can call Melba Strickland to—"

"No," Bella interjected firmly. "Hudson doesn't mind,

and no, you're not staying at Strickland's Boarding House when you've got family here."

He turned his hand over and linked his fingers with hers. "I missed you," he confessed, his voice quiet. "All of you."

"Then why didn't you ever come home?"

He could understand her confusion. She had no way of knowing that his leaving had been prompted not just by grief over the loss of their parents but by guilt—because he was responsible for their being out on the road that night. In addition to all the other factors, that truth was what had compelled him to leave Rust Creek Falls—a futile effort to escape the daily reminders of the mistakes he'd made.

He owed Bella the truth. After all this time, she deserved to know the real reason he went away. But she seemed so happy to see him, and it felt so good to be welcome. The happy light in her eyes warmed the deepest, darkest places in his soul, and Luke didn't want to dim that light.

Not yet.

"You know what? It doesn't matter," she decided when he remained silent. "It only matters that you're here now. And—fingers crossed—Bailey and Liza will soon be, too."

"I don't know if this helps at all, but the last time I saw Bailey, he was heading to New Mexico with his fiancée," Luke said.

"Then Hudson's PI will be heading to New Mexico next," she decided.

"What's in New Mexico?" her husband asked, walking in with a couple of flat boxes in hand.

"Not *what* but *who*," Bella said, lifting her face for his kiss. "And, fingers crossed, the *who* is Bailey."

"New Mexico is a pretty big state," Hudson noted, glancing at Luke. "Any chance you can help narrow down the search?"

Luke shook his head. "Sorry. At the time, I was so baffled by his decision that I didn't ask many questions."

"No worries," Hudson said. "If he's still there, Bradford will find him."

He set the boxes on the table.

Luke sniffed. "Is that…pizza?"

"And wings," Bella told him.

"There's a pizza and wings place in Rust Creek Falls?"

"Wings To Go recently expanded their menu to include pizza." She pushed away from the table and moved to the cupboard to retrieve plates.

"And Daisy's Donut Shop is more than donuts now, too," he noted.

"You've been to Daisy's?" She grabbed a handful of napkins and set them on top of the plates.

"Twice," he admitted. "For coffee on my way to the day care this morning, then for lunch afterward."

"Did you have dessert?"

He shook his head. "The huge roast beef sandwich and mountain of fries filled me up."

"You should have had dessert," Bella said, setting the plates and napkins on the table.

"The woman behind the counter did say that the coconut cream pie was popular," he told her.

"All of the pies, cakes, cookies and pastries are popular," his sister said. "Especially if Eva did the baking."

"Eva?" he echoed, surprised. "The waitress?"

"She sometimes serves customers," Bella confirmed.

"But she does most of the baking at Daisy's. I don't know if she has any formal training, but no one who's tasted any of her creations would question her qualifications as a baker."

"Now I'm sorry I skipped the pie."

"But you got to meet Eva," she noted.

"I guess I did," he agreed.

"She's very pretty, don't you think?"

"I think you need to work on your subtlety," Hudson said to his wife, opening the lid of the pizza box.

"I wasn't trying to be subtle. I was trying to ensure Luke appreciates everything that Rust Creek Falls has to offer."

"I'm not looking for any kind of romantic entanglements while I'm in town," Luke said firmly.

Hudson grinned. "That's what I thought, too, when I first came to Rust Creek Falls."

Chapter Four

Eva had just hung up her apron when the bell above the door jingled. She glanced at Karen, a single mother who worked part-time at the donut shop while her kids were in school. "I have to take off," she told her coworker. "I've got my final exam tonight and I want to review my notes."

"Yeah, I just need a sec," Karen said, not looking up from her phone as her thumbs tapped the keypad. "Sally's at my mom's today, home from school with a fever."

Eva looked longingly toward the promised escape of the back door but, unable to fault the woman's concern for her child, she returned to the front counter.

Her forced smile widened naturally and her heart gave a happy bump inside her chest when it recognized the customer: Luke Stockton.

"Are you here for food or just coffee today?"

"Coffee," he said. "And... I was hoping to see you."

Her heart bumped against her ribs again. "You wanted to see me?"

"Hudson and Bella are both at work today, leaving me alone with my thoughts for the past few hours, and they're really not the best company."

"What were you thinking about?" she asked, filling a ceramic mug from the pot.

"Everything. And nothing." He picked up the mug she set on the counter. "Any chance you can take a break and have a cup of coffee with me?"

"Since I just finished my shift, there's a very good chance," she told him, reaching for a second mug.

Luke carried their beverages to a booth near the window.

Eva slid into the seat across from him. "Do you want to talk about the everything or the nothing?"

He smiled, just a little. "The one very big thing."

"Which is?" she prompted.

"My sister—and my brother, Danny—have asked me to stay in town until his wedding," he confided.

Eva knew—because there were very few secrets in Rust Creek Falls and because the bride had asked her to make the wedding cake—that Danny Stockton and Annie Lattimore were getting married on December twenty-fourth. "It makes sense that he'd want his family to share the occasion," she noted.

"But Christmas Eve is still three weeks away."

"And you have to be back in Wyoming before then?" she guessed.

He shook his head. "No. For the past couple of years, I've been working on a huge spread outside Cheyenne—there are plenty of hands to cover the work, especially this time of year."

"So you could stay...but you don't want to?" she asked, seeking clarification.

"I'm not sure what I want," he admitted. "Bella and Hudson have gone out of their way to make me feel welcome, but it still feels strange to be back after so many years. And I haven't even seen my brother Jamie yet."

Eva remained silent. Though she had a thousand questions she wanted to ask, it was obvious that he needed someone to listen—and not judge.

"He was only fifteen when I left," Luke continued. "Now he's married—for the second time—and the father of three toddlers."

"Henry, Jared and Katie." She opened a packet of sugar and dumped it into her cup, stirred. "They're adorable."

"I guess I'll see for myself this weekend. The invitation to their house came to me through Bella, from Jamie's wife. I'm not even sure if my brother knows that I've been invited."

She lifted her mug and sipped.

"You're not saying much," he noted.

"You haven't actually asked for my opinion on anything," she pointed out.

"Maybe I just needed an ear," he acknowledged. "And a caffeine fix."

"We do have the best coffee in town," she assured him.

"And the best desserts, or so I've heard."

She smiled. "Your sister is a big fan of my brownie bottom cookie dough cheesecake."

"That's probably a little too sweet for my taste, but maybe I will try your apple pie," he decided.

"Sorry," she said sincerely. "It's not on the menu today. But we have key lime and pecan pies, and cherry tarts."

"In that case, I'll try the pecan."

"With salted caramel ice cream or bourbon whipped cream?"

"Bourbon whipped cream sounds interesting," he said.

She slid out of the booth. "Coming right up."

He reached across the table and touched her arm to halt her retreat. It was a casual touch, but the moment his hand brushed her forearm, she felt a jolt of awareness arrow straight to her core. Luke drew his hand away quickly, making her suspect that the shock that had reverberated through her system might have been felt by him, too.

"I thought your shift was finished."

"It is, but—" she glanced toward the counter, where her coworker was unloading a tray of cups with one hand and continuing to text with the other "—Karen's got a lot on her mind right now."

The other woman didn't even look up when Eva moved past her to remove the pie from the case. "How's Sally doing?" she asked as she cut a generous slice and slid it onto a plate.

"Better," Karen said, relief evident in her tone. "The acetaminophen has brought her temperature down, and my mom said she's sipping ginger ale and watching cartoons now."

Eva found the bowl of whipped cream in the refrigerator and added a dollop to Luke's pie.

"Do you want me to deliver that?" her coworker asked. "I thought you said something about needing to study."

"I want to do a final review before the exam, but that shouldn't take too long."

"Well, don't look now," Karen said, "but the handsome cowboy in that booth is studying *you*."

She felt her cheeks flush. "He's just waiting for his dessert."

"He looks like he's got an appetite for something sweet, that's for sure."

Karen was chuckling as Eva hurried away with Luke's

pie. She was pleased that she'd managed to distract the other woman from her worries about her sick child, but she didn't want Luke to be scared off by any speculation or gossip about their personal relationship. Especially when they didn't have a personal relationship—at least not yet. But his admission that he'd come to Daisy's looking for Eva gave her hope.

"Wow," Luke said when she set the plate in front of him. "That's a big slab of pie."

"There are a lot of ranchers in this town," she reminded him. "We're accustomed to serving big appetites."

"Aside from shoveling the driveway—because I didn't know that Hudson had a snowblower—I haven't done much of anything today."

"If the short-term forecast is accurate, you'll be able to shovel again tonight."

"More snow in Montana in December? I'm shocked."

She smiled at that. "Is the weather much different in Wyoming?"

"Not much," he confirmed, sliding a forkful of pie into his mouth, then chewing slowly. "My sister did not exaggerate," he said after he'd swallowed. "This is…damn fine pie."

Eva smiled again, pleased by his reaction. Maybe accounting was a more marketable skill, but she doubted she would ever get as much joy from balancing a ledger as she did from watching a customer enjoy one of her desserts.

And when that customer was as handsome as Luke Stockton, her joy was indescribable.

For the next few minutes he focused his attention on the pie, and Eva sipped her coffee while she pretended not to watch him. Only when his pie was half-eaten, did he speak again.

"One of the other things I've been thinking about is the surprising news I got last night."

"What was that?" she asked him.

"The farm where we grew up—that we assumed would be taken by the bank that held the mortgage—belongs to me and my siblings now."

"And you didn't know?"

He shook his head. "We—at least me and Bailey and Danny—knew that my parents had added to the mortgage to buy some new equipment, so we figured the bank would have taken the property. We didn't know that they'd also added mortgage insurance, and when they were killed, the insurance paid off the money that was owing."

"What about the property taxes?" she wondered.

"Yeah, that's still a big question mark," he admitted.

"You don't know how much is owing?"

"No, we don't know who's been paying them for the past dozen years, but someone has."

"Then there would be a record of the payments at town hall," she pointed out.

"You'd think so," he agreed. "But when Hudson inquired, he was told there's no documentation. No copies of the checks or bank drafts because the payments were cash."

"Cash?" she echoed, surprised.

He nodded. "The taxes aren't small change, either."

"And you have no idea who might have made the payments?"

"None," he confirmed, nudging his plate toward her.

Eva held up a hand, declining his silent offer.

"You know what they say about a chef who doesn't eat her own cooking?" he asked.

"No, I don't. What do they say?"

"I'm not sure," he admitted. "But I think the refusal raises questions about the food."

"So you have questions about my pie?"

Luke chuckled at the indignation in her tone. "Of course not. I'm just asking for help to finish what's left of it."

Sharing his dessert seemed, to Eva, like an intimate act. Was it a sign that he liked her? Or was she reading too much into an innocent offer?

She wanted to believe that his return to Daisy's today was another sign that he was the one, but she was trying not to let her imagination run away with her heart again. Still, she picked up the spoon she'd used to stir sugar into her coffee and scooped up some of the pie.

"What about your grandfather?" she ventured to ask. "Is it possible that he paid the taxes?"

Luke snorted derisively. "He's the last person who would do anything for us."

"Why would you say that?"

"Matthew and Agnes Baldwin made no secret of the fact that they felt overwhelmed by the responsibility of their grandchildren and decided that me, Bailey and Danny—as legal adults—were on our own. That's why we left Rust Creek Falls. What we didn't know then— what I only found out when I came back—was that even four kids were too much for them, and they sent Dana and Liza, our two youngest sisters, away to be adopted."

"I'm so sorry," Eva said sincerely. "I can't imagine how awful that must have been. Not only did you lose your parents, but only weeks later, your family was essentially torn apart, too."

He nodded. "And now Bella has some idealistic notion about putting the pieces back together, and I'm not sure that's even possible. Not after so many years have passed and so many life experiences have separated us."

He scooped up the last bite of pie and offered it to her.

She shook her head. "If you want to make it work, you'll find a way."

"Are you always a glass half-full kind of person?"

"I try to be," she admitted. "So…have you decided whether or not you're going to stay for your brother's wedding?"

"No, but I'm thinking about it," he said.

Karen approached with a fresh pot of coffee in hand. "Refill?"

Luke slid his mug toward her. "Sure. Thanks."

"Eva? An extra kick of caffeine to keep you awake while you're studying?"

She shook her head. "No, thanks. A pot a day is my absolute limit."

Her coworker smiled as she moved away.

Luke sipped his coffee. "What are you studying?"

"I'm taking some online courses toward my accounting degree," she confided.

"You're not really a baker?"

"That's my job—and my passion," she admitted. "But I went to college to study accounting. I'd just finished my first year when my dad got sick." Even now, five years later, she felt the chill right down to her bones to recall the doctor saying the word. "Lymphoma."

"That sucks," Luke said.

She nodded in response to his simple but apt comment.

"The diagnosis was devastating, for all of us. I couldn't imagine going back to school and leaving my mom to deal with all of the doctor appointments and treatment schedules on her own."

"You're an only child?" he guessed.

"No, I've got two older sisters, but they're both married and live out of town."

"So you quit school to help out?"

"I took a leave of absence from my program," she clarified. "But my dad is doing great now—and nagging me to finish my degree. So I've been trying to complete at least one course a term online, and I'm only four courses short now—three, after this term, assuming I pass my final exam."

"And I'm taking you away from your studies."

"I've been studying for the past two weeks."

"Still." He pulled out his wallet and tucked some bills under his plate. "Thanks for your time."

"Thanks for sharing your pie."

He smiled, and she thought that maybe, just maybe, his gaze dropped to her mouth when he said, "Technically it was your pie, but it was my pleasure."

Eva watched him walk toward the door and found herself hoping that she would share a lot more pleasure with the sexy cowboy while he was in town.

Luke had never had any trouble walking away from a woman.

But it was more difficult than he'd expected to slide out of the booth where Eva was still seated and walk out of the donut shop without glancing back.

Maybe it had been a mistake to seek her out, because there was no denying that was exactly what he'd done.

With Bella and Hudson both at the day care, their house had seemed too big and empty, and he'd had no idea what he would do to occupy his time. Then Eva Rose Armstrong's face had popped into his mind, beckoning him with her beautiful blue eyes and welcoming smile.

Not that he was going to "do" the pretty baker, but stopping by Daisy's for a cup of coffee at least gave him an excuse to get out of the house for a while. And to see Eva again.

He couldn't deny that he was drawn to her, and while he wouldn't have said that he had a particular type when it came to the women who caught his eye, he would have said that Eva was definitely *not* his type. She was far too sweet for a man like him. But it was her sweetness that somehow called to him. As if everything that was light and good and whole in her might somehow fix everything that was dark and bad and broken in him.

As if anything could.

Determined to put her out of his mind, he got in his truck and drove. He didn't think he had any particular destination in mind, but a short while later he turned down the familiar gravel drive of what had once been the Sunshine Farm and parked behind Danny's vehicle.

He climbed out of his truck and glanced toward the house but made no move in that direction. While he couldn't deny that he'd been drawn back to the property that had once been his home, he wasn't quite ready to face the memories that waited for him inside the house. Instead, he shifted his attention to the barn—and the Dumpster beside it half-full of old wood and garbage.

Tucking his chin into the collar of his jacket as a defense against the wind, he moved toward the barn, his boots crunching in the snow. There were lights—and heat—inside the barn, and Luke quickly closed the door behind him to keep the cold out and the warmth in.

He found his brother wrestling apart some boards that he recognized as part of a stall enclosure.

"What are you doing?" Luke asked.

Danny paused to wipe the perspiration off his brow with his sleeve. "Building an igloo."

Luke nodded, silently acknowledging the poor wording of his question. "Okay, maybe what I should have asked was 'why are you gutting the barn'?"

"I'm not gutting the whole barn," his brother denied. "Just taking down some of the stall dividers to make room for the chairs."

"Chairs?" he echoed, uncomprehending.

"Annie's got it in her head that this would be the perfect venue for our Christmas Eve wedding."

Luke looked around the dim and undoubtedly aged structure. "Your fiancée wants to get married in a barn?"

"Yep." Danny picked up a sledgehammer again, and another wall partition came down.

"Why?"

"She thinks it will be romantic."

Luke kept his opinion of that to himself as he walked out of the barn and back to his truck to retrieve the heavy-duty work gloves he kept tucked behind the seat with his toolbox.

Danny looked up when he returned. "I thought the mention of romance had scared you off."

Luke began to load up his arms with broken pieces of wood. "I haven't been to a lot of weddings," he acknowledged. "But generally the decor runs to flowers and bows, not cobwebs and dirt."

His brother set down the hammer and bent to pick up

some of the accumulated debris. "I'm getting rid of the cobwebs and dirt to make way for the flowers and bows," he said, following him to the Dumpster.

Luke tossed the wood into the receptacle. "It would be easier to rent the community center."

"I've put a deposit on it," Danny admitted. "Just in case."

"You've done a lot of work already," he noted.

"I can't take credit for all of it. Jamie's been here a few times, Bella and Hudson have also pitched in and Annie's here as much as possible—although I suspect that's as much to ensure I'm following her grand design as to lend a hand."

Luke chuckled. "Spoken like a man who understands his woman."

"I've loved Annie forever, but we could have a hundred years together and I don't think I'd ever pretend to understand her."

"I hope you have a hundred years together to try," he said sincerely.

"You know, that almost sounded like a wedding toast," Danny mused. "Maybe you can repeat it on the twenty-fourth with a glass in your hand."

"I haven't decided if I'm going to stay that long," he reminded his brother.

"I know," Danny acknowledged. "But even if you don't stay, you could come back for the wedding. I'd really like you to be there."

"Then I will be," he decided. "Even if I don't stay, I'll be here on the big day."

"Of course, if you stay, you could help me turn this place into a wedding venue."

"I'm a ranch hand, bro, not a miracle worker."

Danny chuckled as they both got back to work.

But while Luke continued to ferry broken boards and debris to the Dumpster, he thought that maybe he would stay.

And maybe he would spend some time with Eva Armstrong while he was in town.

Chapter Five

A day off from the donut shop usually meant sleeping in for Eva, but she was awake early Saturday morning. She had too many things on her mind to be able to linger in bed. Or maybe it was too much of one thing on her mind—Luke Stockton.

She hadn't stopped thinking about the man since he stepped up to the counter at Daisy's on his first day back in town and ordered his coffee. Large. Black. To go. It wasn't really the way he drank his coffee that stuck in her mind— it was the low, rumbling tone of his voice, the intensity in his deep blue eyes, the sexy curve of his unsmiling lips, the strong line of his jaw, the breadth of his shoulders and—

She shook her head.

And she was pathetically infatuated with a man she'd only crossed paths with a few times.

But in her heart, she was sure that Luke's return to Rust Creek Falls now, after a dozen years away, was destiny. And after more failed relationships than she wanted to acknowledge, she believed that fate had deliberately put him in her path.

Of course, fate had given her signals before—inaccurate

and unreliable ones. But Eva refused to give up. She believed in true love and happily-ever-after, and she trusted—with all of her heart—that she would find hers.

After a quick shower, she went downstairs for a cup of the coffee she knew her mother would have left on the warmer. Since her father's cancer diagnosis, her parents had vowed to live every minute to the fullest. As a result, it was rare for them to spend time just hanging out around the house. Today they'd planned to leave early for Kalispell to browse the antiques shops; then they were having dinner with friends in the city, which meant that Eva had most of the day and the house all to herself.

As she sipped her first cup of coffee, she gathered the ingredients for her not-quite-famous, melt-in-your-mouth pie crust. Because a day off from the donut shop didn't mean a day away from the kitchen. In fact, she was never happier than when she was mixing and measuring.

From an early age, she'd been fascinated by the process of putting together various dry and wet ingredients. Maybe they didn't look like much of anything before they were put in the oven, but somehow, as she watched through the glass window, magic happened, turning unappealing pans of goop and lumps of batter into the most delicious cakes and cookies that brought smiles to the faces of her family and friends. By the time she was old enough to understand that it wasn't magic but heat that caused the transformation, it didn't matter—she was hooked.

As she cut the butter into the flour, the bowl of glossy red apples on the table snagged her attention. Well, that made the decision easy. She would make an apple pie. Not because Luke happened to mention that he was "an apple pie kind of guy" but because she had the necessary ingredients on hand.

She peeled and sliced the apples—enough for two pies, so that her mother could serve one for dessert after Sunday dinner.

Then she squeezed lemon juice over the fruit, sprinkled on some cinnamon and a light dusting of flour, then tossed the apples to ensure they were evenly coated.

Setting that bowl aside, she floured her work surface and rolled out the pastry she'd mixed earlier. She divided the filling between two dishes, then cut strips of rolled-out pastry to make the basket-weave crust, laid it over the apples, trimmed and pinched the edges, then sprinkled the top with sugar and slid the glass pie plates into the oven.

She tidied up the kitchen and sat down at the table with a second cup of coffee to wonder what she was going to do with the rest of her day. Of course, her thoughts then wandered to wondering what Luke Stockton was doing.

When the scent of baking apples began to permeate the air, she looked up Hudson Jones's phone number and impulsively dialed. As she listened to the ring, she felt butterflies fluttering in her belly. Maybe this was a mistake. It was certainly presumptuous. The man had simply made a throwaway comment about apple pie and—

"Hello?"

She immediately recognized Luke's sister's voice. "Hi, Bella, it's Eva Armstrong—from Daisy's Donut Shop."

"Hi, Eva." The other woman's tone was friendly enough, but Eva could hear the unspoken question in her response.

"I hope I'm not interrupting anything, but I'm trying to reach your brother, Luke."

"Luke?" Bella echoed, sounding even more surprised now.

"When he was at the donut shop the other day, he mentioned that he liked apple pie and I baked one this morning that I could drop off for him."

"He does like apple pie," Bella confirmed.

"Should I bring it over, then?"

"I wish I could say yes and maybe steal a slice for myself," his sister said, "but Luke's actually at Short Hills Ranch visiting Jamie and Fallon and the kids today."

"Oh." Eva felt her spirits sink along with the possibility of crossing paths with the handsome cowboy.

"Of course, Jamie has a sweet tooth, too," Bella told her. "If you wanted to take a drive over to the ranch, I'm sure your pie would be devoured and appreciated there."

"I don't want to intrude on their reunion," she protested.

"I'm sure Luke would be happy to see you. Maybe even relieved."

"Relieved?" she echoed.

"I know Jamie's glad that Luke came home," Bella explained. "But I'm not sure he's quite ready to forgive him for leaving in the first place."

"He must have had his reasons," Eva ventured, recalling what he'd told her about the situation after their parents were killed.

"Do you know where Short Hills Ranch is?" Bella asked her now.

"I do," Eva confirmed. "But—"

"Good." The other woman cut off her objection. "It would be a shame for that pie to go to waste."

And Eva let Luke's sister's words convince her.

Luke might have grown up with six younger siblings, but he'd had little-to-no contact with kids in recent years.

And while he'd been looking forward to seeing Jamie again and meeting his brother's little ones, he couldn't deny that he was feeling a little overwhelmed.

The toddlers were so active and boisterous, it was hard to believe that they'd been preemies. Maybe Henry, Jared and Katie were still small for twenty-two months—since he had no idea what was the average height or weight of an almost two-year-old, he'd take Fallon's word for that—but they were undoubtedly healthy and happy. And loud. Very loud.

Which wasn't entirely a bad thing as their non-stop chatter filled the long gaps and uncomfortable silences that punctuated his attempts at conversation with his youngest brother. Fallon tried to help, introducing topics that she thought might establish some common ground. But it was obvious to Luke that his brother was still angry—and maybe even hurt—by what he considered the abandonment by his three older siblings almost a dozen years earlier.

And though Jamie had apparently welcomed Daniel with open arms when he'd returned to Rust Creek Falls, Luke understood why his youngest brother might harbor more resentment toward him. As the oldest, Luke was the one who could have—and maybe should have—taken the initiative to look after his siblings and keep them all together. Instead, he'd failed them all.

The dogs provided another welcome distraction from the awkwardness between the brothers. In addition to three babies, Jamie had two retriever-shepherd mix puppies that were just over a year old. And the adorable mutts, like the kids, held nothing back.

According to Fallon, Jamie had found the pups the previous winter. The mother had been hit by a car and

Jamie had rounded up her babies—seven in total—and taken them to the vet to be checked over and placed in good homes. Jamie hadn't intended to keep even one for himself, but he'd somehow ended up bringing two of them home.

Andy and Molly had barked like crazy when Luke showed up at the door, jumping all over one another in their efforts to be the first to greet the visitor. A quick word from Jamie, however, and they'd immediately dropped their butts to the floor, although their bodies had continued to quiver with repressed excitement.

There was nothing repressed about them now as they tumbled on the floor with the kids, rewarding tugs on their ears and tails with sloppy, wet kisses. Growing up on Sunshine Farm, there had always been at least one dog around, but over the years, Luke had forgotten how much comfort and companionship an animal could provide. Maybe when he got back to Cheyenne he could drop by the shelter and pick out a dog. The idea was incredibly appealing to him, but he suspected a dog wouldn't be happy confined in a tiny apartment while his human companion was gone from sunup to sundown every day.

"Are you getting hungry, Luke?" Fallon's question drew him back to the present.

"*I'm* hungry," her husband interjected.

"You're always hungry," she said, but she softened the reproach with a smile that was filled with love and affection.

Luke looked away, deliberately refocusing his attention on the babies so that he didn't feel like a voyeur.

Maybe he shouldn't stay in Rust Creek Falls too long. Both of his siblings who had remained in town—and the one who had returned—had fallen in love, and he had no desire to walk down the same path. He'd already experienced enough heartache to last a lifetime.

Sure, it warmed his heart to see Bella with Hudson, and to witness the way her millionaire husband doted on her. And yeah, he could appreciate the obvious connection between Jamie and Fallon—and no doubt Jamie appreciated having not just an extra set of hands to help with his three babies but the partnership of a woman who clearly loved Henry, Jared and Katie as if they were her own.

The engagement of Danny and Annie was less surprising to Luke, because he remembered how deeply in love his brother had been before they left town. In fact, Danny was the only one who had balked about the decision to leave Rust Creek Falls, and Luke had always suspected that Annie was the reason.

"I'm just going to check on the bread that's in the oven," Fallon said at the same time the doorbell rang. "Were you expecting more company?" she asked her husband.

Jamie shook his head.

"Bella?" Luke guessed as Henry climbed up onto the sofa and then onto his uncle's shoulders from there. He instinctively reached up to hold the boy steady, not wanting to be responsible for the little guy tumbling off and crashing to the ground.

"She lived here with me and the triplets for more than fifteen months—she rarely remembers to knock before walking in," Jamie responded, but there was affection rather than disapproval in his tone.

Jared—eager to do everything his brother did—was attempting to crawl up Luke's front. "I'm glad you and

Bella stayed close," Luke said as he steadied the second toddler.

"We had to," Jamie said pointedly. "We were all that we each had left."

Luke didn't know how to respond to that. No matter how many times he apologized, it wouldn't change what had happened when he'd left Rust Creek Falls—or the reasons he'd felt compelled to go. Nothing could change the past, so he'd learned to put one foot in front of the other and move forward, though the weight of the guilt and regrets made the progress painfully slow.

He was grateful when Fallon came back into the family room, and even more so when he realized that she wasn't alone.

"Look who dropped by," she said.

Luke did look, and he felt an immediate pull low in his belly when he saw Eva Armstrong. He recognized the pull as basic physical attraction, and while he was willing to acknowledge that his blood hummed in his veins whenever he was near the pretty baker, he was also determined to ignore the hormones clamoring for him to stop looking and start moving.

"Bella told me that you'd be here," Eva explained before anyone could ask. "I didn't want to interrupt but—"

"You're not interrupting anything," Luke interjected, inexplicably grateful for her presence.

"Eva brought pie," Fallon said. "Still-warm-from-the-oven apple pie."

"My favorite," Luke noted.

Eva's cheeks flushed with pretty color. "Yes, you mentioned that when you were at Daisy's the other day."

"You made the pie for me?" he asked, surprised and pleased by the gesture.

She shrugged. "I like to bake, and I had apples on hand."

"If only we had ice cream," Jamie lamented as his daughter toddled over to their new guest and lifted her arms in a silent plea to be picked up.

Eva, without any hesitation, did so, propping the toddler on her hip with a natural ease that Luke couldn't help but envy. "I brought some of that, too," she said.

"Then I say it's time for pie," Jamie said.

Luke, his mouth already watering in anticipation—for Eva as much as her pie—nodded his agreement.

But Fallon shook her head. "We can have pie for dessert *after* lunch, which I am going to dish up now."

"That's my cue to go," Eva said, but Katie was winding a strand of Eva's long blond hair around her hand, effectively entangling her.

The neat braid she'd worn when she was working behind the counter at Daisy's was pretty enough and undoubtedly practical for work, but Luke liked the way she looked now, with her hair tumbling over her shoulders—and captured in his adorable niece's fist.

"But you just got here," Luke protested.

"And it's lunchtime," she pointed out.

"You can stay and eat with us," Fallon said. "There's plenty to go around."

"Oh, no, I couldn't," Eva said.

"Do you have other plans?" Jamie's wife asked her.

"No," she admitted. "But I really don't want to intrude."

"You're really not," Fallon assured her. "I'll just go set another place at the table."

"Are you sure you don't mind?" Eva asked, her gaze sliding to Luke as if gauging his reaction.

"Of course not," Fallon insisted.

"My wife always cooks enough for several extra people," Jamie said. "And her beef stew is exceptional."

"Beef stew sounds like the perfect meal to warm the blood on a cold day," Eva said.

Luke was pretty sure he knew at least a dozen more interesting ways to warm her blood, but he quickly slammed the door on that wayward thought.

"Then let's get HJK rounded up and settled into their high chairs for lunch," Jamie said, lifting Jared off his brother's chest and into the air, making the little guy giggle.

"Up! Up!" Henry demanded.

Fallon deftly took Jared from her husband so that he could treat Henry to the same high ride.

Since Eva already had Katie on her hip, she carried the little girl to the kitchen.

Luke followed, appreciating the subtle sway of her hips beneath the long, loose skirt. Most of the women he knew lived in jeans and flannel, but Eva seemed to prefer softer fabrics and styles. Rather than downplay her femininity, she embraced it. And Luke found himself wanting to embrace it, too, and every other part of her.

Eva felt a little self-conscious about sitting down with the Stocktons for what was obviously a family meal, but everyone else seemed to take her presence in stride. Fallon directed her to the empty chair beside Luke, but first, Eva set Katie in her high chair, buckling the belt around her middle to ensure the active toddler wouldn't be able to wriggle out of it.

Jamie dampened a cloth under the faucet, then made his way from one high chair to the next, thoroughly scrubbing all the little hands in what was obviously a pre-dining ritual. Although Fallon had only been married to the triplets' father for about seven months, Eva knew that Jamie's bride had been involved in caring for Henry, Jared and Katie since they were born.

After the babies' biological mother died from complications of childbirth, several residents of Rust Creek Falls had volunteered to form a "baby chain" to help the new father care for his three premature infants. As a result of Fallon's participation in the baby chain, she and her new husband already had well-established routines for the care of their little ones. And although the toddlers had only just met their uncle, Eva could tell that they had immediately taken a liking to Luke.

No doubt he would be a good father to his own children someday—a thought that brought to mind an image of chubby-cheeked babies with Luke's deep blue eyes and dark blond hair. Or maybe lighter hair, more like her own.

Eva pushed the tantalizing picture to the back of her mind, ruefully acknowledging that it was a little premature to be thinking about having babies with a man who hadn't even kissed her.

But it was going to happen.

The kiss, at least—she was sure of it.

Not that her recent dating history had given her any reason for such optimism. In fact, just the opposite was true. While it seemed as if everyone she knew was falling in love, getting married and having babies—although not always in that order—Eva was still alone.

In the past few years, she'd gone out with a few different guys—and two that seemed to have real potential. She'd dated Bobby Ray Ellis for a few months before she realized that he was still in love with his high school sweetheart—even years after she'd moved out of town and married someone else. Then Zach Dalton moved to Rust Creek Falls, and Eva had been certain that he was the one. Unfortunately, as much as she wanted the relationship to work, she had to admit there'd been zero chemistry between them. Which didn't make it hurt any less when she was dumped—again.

But she continued to trust that she would know her soul mate when she found him—as had happened for her parents and her sisters. Her dad, a young history teacher losing a battle with the school photocopier, had been rescued by the new office administrator. According to Ray Armstrong, Marion Barr had simultaneously saved his test papers and stolen his heart. Six months later, they were married.

Both of Eva's sisters had also been lucky in love. Calla met her husband, Patrick, when she was seventeen years old and on a high school ski trip in Thunder Canyon. Delphine met her husband, Harrison, at college.

Eva only wanted the same thing both of her sisters had—a husband, a family. But she was a twenty-five-year-old single woman who hadn't had a date since she'd been jilted by Zach Dalton. Still, the flutters that tickled her belly whenever she saw Luke Stockton gave her hope that might change.

"Bread?" the object of her musings asked, offering the basket that Fallon had set on the table.

"Thanks." She selected a slice and passed the basket to Jamie.

She felt something rub against her ankle and, for a moment, thought it might be Luke's foot. Then she felt the weight of a paw on her toes and realized the dogs were under the table, no doubt hoping that someone would drop—accidentally or on purpose—scraps for them.

She wasn't the only one aware of their presence, either, because Fallon tipped her head to peer under the table. "Andy, Molly—go lie down."

The dogs obediently followed her command, their ears and tails drooping in response to the scolding. Henry dropped a piece of bread as the animals moved past his high chair, which one of the pups snatched up before any of the humans could do so.

"I almost forgot to ask," Luke said to her. "How was your exam?"

"I think it went pretty well," she said cautiously.

"Now only three more courses to go and you'll be an accountant," he noted.

She was surprised that he'd remembered the details of their conversation about her studies, even if he was jumping the gun a little. "I'll have a degree," she clarified. "There are more exams after that before I'll actually be certified."

"I didn't know you wanted to be an accountant," Fallon chimed in.

"Truthfully, I'd rather bake cookies than crunch numbers, but I've been told that accounting is a more marketable skill."

"If you become a CPA, who will fill the pastry case at Daisy's?" Luke wondered.

She shrugged. "Anyone who can read can follow a recipe."

"*Almost* anyone," Jamie said, his lips twitching as he shared a look with his wife.

"It happened *once*," she said, then turned to explain to Eva. "*One time* I mixed up teaspoons and tablespoons."

"What were you measuring?"

"Baking powder," Fallon admitted.

Eva winced.

The other woman sighed. "Yeah, it was pretty bad."

"But this stew is delicious," Eva told her, dipping her spoon into the bowl again.

"I've learned to stick with what I know," Fallon said.

For the next few minutes everyone showed their appreciation for the meal by focusing on eating.

Although there wasn't a lot of conversation at the table, Eva did notice that Luke's occasional questions to his brother were met by sharp and succinct responses followed by silence. She didn't know Jamie Stockton well enough to know if he was always a man of few words or if he didn't have much to say to his brother, but his wife's obvious efforts to fill in the gaps made Eva suspect that it was the latter.

Maybe it wasn't surprising that, after so many years apart, there would be some residual tension between the siblings, but she hoped they could work it out because she suspected there was little chance of Luke deciding to stay in Rust Creek Falls if they didn't.

Chapter Six

By the time lunch was finished—including Eva's apple pie for dessert—the little ones were practically falling asleep in their high chairs. Fallon and Jamie excused themselves to get Henry, Jared and Katie washed up and settled down for their naps, and Eva and Luke tidied the kitchen.

"Was that as awkward for you as it was for me?" Luke asked as he carried a stack of bowls from the table to the counter.

"There were a few awkward moments," Eva acknowledged.

"At least I learned something about my youngest brother today that I didn't know before."

"What's that?" she wondered, dividing the cutlery between the basket compartments in the dishwasher.

"He sure does know how to hold on to a grudge."

"You've been gone for twelve years," Eva reminded him. "You can't expect to pick up right where you left off."

"I didn't have any expectations." He squirted dish soap into the sink and began to fill it with hot water.

"Are you sure about that?" she asked, slotting the bowls on the bottom rack.

He frowned. "What do you mean?"

"It just seems, at least to this outside observer, that you expected a less-than-warm welcome, and that's exactly what you got."

"A self-fulfilling prophecy?"

"Maybe," she allowed, closing the dishwasher.

He slid the pots and pans into the soapy water. "Well, I'm glad you were here—and not just because you brought dessert, although that was a definite bonus."

"I'm glad, too," she said. "I like your family."

"Tell me about yours," he suggested. "You mentioned that you have two sisters—where do they live?"

"Calla lives in Thunder Canyon, where she helps her husband, Patrick, run his hardware store. They have two kids—Fiona, who is almost ten, and Noah, who just turned seven.

"Delphine lives a little farther away, in Billings. She's a middle school teacher, married to a financial adviser. She and Harrison have three boys—eight-year-old Tommy, six-year-old Charlie and four-year-old Freddy."

"So you have a lot of experience with kids," he noted.

She shook her head. "Not nearly as much as I would like. Aside from major holidays, I rarely get to see my niece and nephews."

"But I bet you spoil them rotten when you do."

"Absolutely," she agreed. "Their Christmas presents are stacked almost floor to ceiling in my room."

"You've started your Christmas shopping already?"

"Haven't you?"

He shook his head. "I still haven't decided if I'm going to be here for Christmas."

"What does that have to do with your shopping?" she asked.

"If I'm not here, I won't need to buy any presents," he said logically.

Eva was taken aback. Not just by the statement but by his matter-of-fact tone. "There's no one else you celebrate the holidays with?"

"No."

She frowned at that. "So what do you usually do on December twenty-fifth?"

"The same thing I do on the twenty-fourth and the twenty-sixth."

"For the past twelve years, you haven't done anything to celebrate Christmas?"

"Well, some of the bigger spreads put out a fancy meal for their hands," he told her.

She was silent for a moment, not knowing what to say. Her heart ached for him, but she knew he would balk at any expression of sympathy.

"If you decide to stay, I could help you with your shopping," she finally said.

"I appreciate the offer, but I'm not sure even your company would make up for having to set foot in a mall."

"I love Christmas shopping. And wrapping presents, and trimming the tree. And holiday baking, of course."

"How is holiday baking different from regular baking?" he wondered aloud.

She smiled. "There's a lot more of it. Cookies and squares and bars. And, of course, Christmas goodies don't have any calories."

"No calories, huh?"

"Nope. Not even my absolutely decadent chocolate

almond macaroon bars, which means that I'm free to indulge."

"If your chocolate almond macaroon bars are half as good as your pies, I'd want to indulge, too," he told her. "In fact, I'm seriously considering taking a fork and eating what's left of that apple pie directly from the dish before my brother and sister-in-law come back down."

"I'm sure they'll let you take the leftovers with you."

"Then I'd have to share with Bella and Hudson," he grumbled as he wiped off the trays of the high chairs, which had been liberally smeared with beef gravy and vanilla ice cream by toddler hands.

Eva chuckled as she picked up a towel to dry the trays after he'd finished cleaning them. "I could probably bake another one sometime."

He returned to the sink to rinse the cloth, then began to tackle the pots and pans. "I would think, on your day off, you'd want to stay out of the kitchen."

She shrugged. "I like baking. The rhythm of measuring and mixing is relaxing to me."

"Do you cook, too?" he asked her, scrubbing the inside of the stew pot.

"Of course," she said, then glanced at him over her shoulder as she slid the high chairs back against the wall. "Are you angling for a meal?"

"No," he said quickly. Then he reconsidered, lifting one shoulder and offering her a half smile. "Maybe."

She chuckled. "How about dinner on Tuesday?"

"Really? You would cook dinner for me?"

"Sure."

He set the clean pot in the dish drainer and turned to face her. "I don't have any specific plans this week, so

Tuesday works for me," he finally said. "But I have to admit that I'm curious."

"About what?"

"Why you'd offer to feed a man you barely know."

"Because sharing a meal will give us the opportunity to get to know one another better," she pointed out.

"That it would," he agreed cautiously.

"How's six o'clock?" she suggested.

"Six is fine, but…"

She looked up, waiting for him to complete what was obviously an unfinished thought.

"But?" she prompted when he remained silent.

"I'm not looking for any kind of romantic entanglement while I'm in town," he finally responded. "And I feel really stupid even saying that because maybe your offer to cook dinner is nothing more than that, but I just want to be sure there's no misunderstanding."

"I appreciate that," she said, picking up the pot to dry it. "Are you involved with somebody in Cheyenne?"

He shook his head. "No."

"Somewhere else?"

"No," he said again. "I don't do relationships."

She took a minute to consider that response before she said, "I have just one more question."

"What's that?" he asked warily.

"Do you like pot roast?"

He grinned. "Does a cowboy wear a hat?"

She smiled back. "Then I'll see you at six on Tuesday."

As Luke stood at the door, hand poised to knock, it belatedly occurred to him that he should have brought something. Flowers or a bottle of wine, maybe. As he honestly couldn't remember the last time a woman had offered to cook a meal for him, he was unfamiliar with the usual procedures and protocols. And if he'd brought flowers or wine, it might have seemed too much like a date, and it wasn't. He was looking forward to sharing a meal with Eva, but he wasn't looking for anything more than that.

That conviction flew right out of his head when she greeted him with a genuine and warm smile on her face, and he suddenly realized that he wanted to kiss her more than he'd wanted anything else in a very long time.

"Good—you're on time," she said.

"You said six," he reminded her, his gaze lingering on the sweet curve of her mouth.

"And you heard," she noted, stepping back from the door so that he could enter.

He barely had a moment to look at her—the long, flowing skirt that swirled around her calves and soft pink sweater that hugged her feminine curves—before she was moving away again.

"Hang up your coat there—" she gestured to a row of hooks on the wall beside the door "—then come on into the kitchen. I was just about to start slicing the beef."

He inhaled the scent of savory roasted meat and his stomach immediately rumbled. He unzipped his jacket and hung it on one of the empty hooks on the wall, then put his Stetson on top of it. There was a bench seat beneath the row of hooks, and he sat down to remove his snowy boots before following the path Eva had taken through the foyer and into the kitchen.

He would have guessed—based on the design and the neighborhood—that the house was close to forty years old, but this room had recently been updated. With white shaker-style cabinets, dark gray granite countertops and stainless-steel appliances, it was sleek and modern and spotlessly clean.

The farmhouse table was already set with dark blue placemats and linen napkins that contrasted against simple white dinnerware. There was a bottle of wine on the table, already open, and two glasses waiting.

Not a date, he reminded himself, though the setting suggested otherwise. The only things missing were candles and flowers. Or maybe he was reading too much into her preparations.

"This is your place?" he asked, surprised that a young, single woman would choose to rent a house rather than an apartment—and that she could afford such accommodations.

Eva shook her head. "It's my parents' house."

"Where do they live?" he wondered.

"Here."

"You still live with your parents?"

Her gaze dropped away and her cheeks flushed. "For now."

"I didn't mean to imply that there's anything wrong with that," he said.

"I moved out a few years ago, when I went to college," she confided.

"But you came back when your dad was diagnosed," he remembered. Which was almost the same thing Bella had done, putting her education on hold to help Jamie with his triplets after the death of his first wife.

Eva nodded.

"I'm sorry," he said, feeling as if he'd stuck one of his enormous feet into his mouth. And despite the two place settings on the table, he had to ask, "Is this a... family dinner?"

She laughed softly. "No. I wouldn't do that to you—to anyone," she assured him.

He exhaled, immeasurably relieved by her response. A homemade meal with a pretty woman was one thing—meeting the parents of a girl he wasn't even dating was something entirely different.

"My parents are out tonight. In fact, they're out every Tuesday and Thursday night."

Which, he suspected, was why she'd chosen to invite him for dinner tonight.

"Since my dad finished his treatments, he and my mom decided they weren't going to take anything for granted or put off doing something they wanted to do for another day, because there are no guarantees of other days."

That was a lesson Luke had learned, too, the night his parents were killed.

He pushed the past aside to focus on the present.

"So they joined a couples' bowling league in Kalispell, they take ballroom dance lessons at the community center and they have regular date nights. Tonight is one of those dates, and they've gone to Kalispell for dinner and a movie."

"Still no movie theater in Rust Creek Falls?" he guessed.

"Just the high school gym on Friday and Saturday nights—and only so long as none of the varsity teams is playing."

"Go Wildcats," he said, and made her laugh again.

"So what do your parents think about you having a man in the house while they're away?" he teased.

She carried the platter of meat to the table. "I didn't tell them I was having company for dinner," she admitted.

"Why not?" he asked, following with the bowls of mashed potatoes and mixed vegetables.

"Because my parents tend to be a little…overprotective," she said as she poured gravy into a ceramic pitcher.

He lifted the bottle of merlot—a silent question. She nodded, and he poured the wine into their glasses.

"Probably because you don't have any older brothers to look out for you."

"Did you look out for your younger sisters?"

It was an innocent question—and one that flowed naturally from their topic of conversation—but it brought the harsh realities rushing back to him. "Not as much as I should have in the early years," he acknowledged. "And then I lost the chance to do so."

She touched a hand to his arm. "I'm sorry. I didn't mean to bring up unhappy memories."

He pulled away from her touch, not wanting or deserving her comfort, and picked up his fork, slicing easily through the beef on his plate. "Wow. This is so tender I barely need the knife." He took a taste and savored the bite. "Mmm. And juicy."

She acknowledged his compliment—and the change of topic—with a slight nod. "I hope Bella doesn't mind that you're not there for dinner tonight."

"Are you kidding? She decided it was a good excuse not to cook so Hudson was taking her out to eat."

"Maverick Manor?" she guessed.

"I didn't ask," he admitted, then frowned. "Is that the fancy new hotel on the highway headed toward Kalispell?"

She nodded.

"Good food there?"

"That's the rumor," she told him. "Although I couldn't say for sure, because I've never been."

"Why not?" Noting that her glass was almost empty, he lifted the bottle to top up her drink but didn't add to his own because he had a hard and fast rule about never consuming more than a single alcoholic beverage when he was driving.

"It's not exactly the type of place where a woman would go on her own—even if she could afford it," Eva said in response to his question.

He shook his head as he swallowed the last bite of his meal. "What's wrong with the guys in this town that none of them has offered to take you?"

"That's a question you'd have to ask them," she said.

Though the smile remained on her face, her tone was a little stiff, and Luke mentally cursed himself for his insensitivity. She was a gorgeous woman who worked magic in the kitchen, so he'd naturally assumed her unmarried status was a matter of choice. Apparently, he was wrong.

"Did you leave room for dessert?" Eva pushed away from the table and carried their plates to the counter. "I made gingerbread and white chocolate mousse trifle."

"I would have said I couldn't eat another bite, but that sounds too delicious to resist," he told her.

"Do you want coffee with dessert?"

"I always want coffee—if it's not too much trouble," he said.

"No trouble at all," she assured him, reaching for the carafe. Then as he opened the dishwasher, she asked, "What are you doing?"

He started to load the dishes she had cleared from

the table. "Helping with the cleanup," he said, in case it wasn't obvious.

"You're not supposed to do that," she protested.

"Why not?"

"Because you're a guest."

"You were a guest at Jamie and Fallon's, but you insisted on helping."

"I was an *uninvited* guest," she pointed out. "And Jamie and Fallon had their hands full with the kids."

"My mom always said that a man could best show his appreciation for a meal by helping with the cleanup afterward."

"In that case, I will stop protesting and say thank you."

"Thank *you*," Luke said. "That was truly the best meal I've had in a long time. Of course, if you tell my sister or sister-in-law I said that, I'll deny it till the cows come home."

"I would never," she promised.

He closed the dishwasher. "Trifle?"

"Coming right up."

As much as Eva enjoyed being in the kitchen, she got even more pleasure watching others enjoy her creations, so she was thrilled when Luke finished off two servings of trifle. Except that when he set his spoon inside the empty bowl, it was a definite signal that dinner was over.

"More coffee?" she offered.

He shook his head as he glanced at the clock over the sink. "No, thanks. I should probably be heading back."

He pushed away from the table, gathered her bowl along with his own and carried them to the dishwasher. Eva followed with their empty coffee mugs.

Luke turned as she approached the dishwasher, so she

stepped to the side—and he did the same. She moved to the other side—and he did the same again.

"Dinner *and* dancing," he noted.

She smiled as she shifted again.

This time he tried to get out of her way by moving forward and she bumped into him. Or rather the mugs she carried bumped into his chest. His broad, solid, warm chest.

"You really need to stop trying to lead," he teased.

"It's the music," she bantered back.

He took the mugs from her hands and turned to set them in the top rack of the machine, then closed the door.

Eva didn't move. She was too preoccupied with the alluring view of well-worn denim stretching across his nicely curved backside.

Then he turned again and straightened, so that her gaze was now fixed on that strong chest. She lifted her eyes to his broad shoulders, the shadow of stubble on his jaw, the sensual curve of his lips.

Those lips were moving now, so she made an effort to focus on his words rather than speculate about how his mouth would feel against hers.

"It was kind of you to invite me for dinner tonight. Thank you," he said.

"You're very welcome."

Neither of them moved.

His gaze dropped to her mouth, for just a second, then jerked away. Almost as if he'd been thinking about kissing her before he remembered that he didn't want to get involved. But there had been so much intensity in that brief moment, Eva's breath backed up in her lungs and her knees actually quivered.

She moistened her lips with the tip of her tongue. "Luke."

She didn't say anything other than his name, but she suspected that single syllable told him everything she was thinking and feeling. His response confirmed it.

"Don't look at me like that," he warned.

"Like what?"

"Like you're wishing I would kiss you."

Was it the wine that made her brave? Or was it not knowing how long he was going to be in town that made her reluctant to waste any time playing games?

"Maybe I am wishing you would kiss me," she told him.

He shook his head, sincerely regretful. "It's not going to happen, Eva."

Her hopes fizzled like a balloon leaking air. "You don't want to kiss me?"

"It's not about what I want. It's about what's smart," he said.

"And kissing me wouldn't be smart?" she guessed.

"I have no business getting involved with you—with anyone—when I'm only going to be in Rust Creek Falls for a few weeks."

"So you've said," she noted.

"I just want to be clear. I came back because Bella was looking for me, but I'm not planning to stay."

"I don't think that's the only reason you came back," she said. "I think you wanted to see your siblings as much as they wanted to see you."

"Maybe I did," he acknowledged. "That doesn't change the fact that my life is in Wyoming now."

"Okay," she said agreeably.

Then she took another half step forward so that she

was standing even closer to him now, and tipped her chin up to meet his gaze.

"What are you doing?" he asked a little warily.

"Since you've made it clear that you have no intention of kissing me, I'm going to have to take matters into my own hands."

Then she lifted those hands to his shoulders, rose up onto her toes and touched her mouth to his.

Chapter Seven

It was a casual kiss. Barely a brush of her lips against his, but the effect was like touching a lit match to dry tinder, and desire flamed hot and bright inside her. Maybe inside him, too. Because before she could draw away, his arm was at her back, hauling her against him.

And then *he* was kissing *her*.

She might have initiated the contact, but Luke quickly took over. Eva was happy to relinquish control because, wow, did he know how to kiss.

His lips were warm and firm and moved over hers with just the right amount of pressure. When his tongue traced the seam of her lips, she parted willingly to let him inside.

For a man who claimed that he had no business getting involved, he was definitely involved in the kiss. And when his hands slid up her back, urging her even closer, she linked her hands behind his neck and held on while the world shifted beneath her feet.

She didn't know how long the kiss went on, except that it was long enough to melt all the bones in her body and completely blank her mind. She could think of nothing but Luke, want nothing but Luke. And even when her brain registered a quiet chime somewhere in the distance, it was several seconds later before she recognized the sound.

Luke eased his lips from hers and exhaled slowly. "That must be yours."

"My what?"

"Phone," he said.

"Oh. Right."

Eva drew an unsteady breath and tried to remember where she'd left her phone. She found it in the pocket of her coat.

"My parents," she explained, after she'd unlocked the screen and read the message. "They always send a quick text to let me know when they're on their way home."

"I guess that's my cue to be heading out."

"There's no need to rush off," she protested.

He moved toward the door and sat on the bench to stuff his feet into his boots again.

"Thanks. I really enjoyed dinner." His gaze dropped to her mouth, and his own lips curved. "And dessert."

Eva's cheeks turned pink but she seemed to accept his words at face value. "I'll get the rest of the trifle for you to take with you."

"I should tell you not to bother, but it was really good."

She laughed softly as she went to retrieve the leftover dessert from the refrigerator.

And yeah, he watched her cross the kitchen floor, admiring the nicely rounded curve of her butt as she moved.

There was no point in denying that he was attracted to her. And why wouldn't he be? She was pretty and spunky, and the sweet, seductive flavor of her lips made him want a lot more.

It had been a while since he'd enjoyed intimate female companionship. He couldn't remember how long exactly—three months? Four? Longer?

There was a woman who worked as a bartender at his favorite watering hole in Cheyenne. A curvy brunette who was amenable to hooking up when they were both in the mood. He hadn't been in the mood in a while. Truthfully, he hadn't even thought about her in months. And he suspected that, if asked, she would say the same about him.

Which was probably why he was so strongly attracted to Eva. She was a beautiful woman and he was a red-blooded man who had been sleeping alone for a long time. If the pretty baker was willing to help him end that period of self-imposed celibacy, he would be crazy to turn her down. Especially when he wanted nothing more than to peel away her clothes as if they were one of those paper cupcake liners, then lick her all over as if her body was covered in buttercream icing.

"I'm glad you enjoyed it," Eva said as she walked back to him.

It took his brain a minute to shake off the fantasy and recall the topic of their conversation. "I did," he said, accepting the bowl she offered.

Then, almost of its own volition, his free hand lifted to cup her cheek, his thumb brushing lightly over the curve of her bottom lip.

"You're a tempting woman, Eva Armstrong." And though he couldn't deny that he wanted her, he forced his hand to drop away. "But I can't afford to give in to temptation."

Once again, she surprised him. Instead of accepting the boundary he was attempting to establish, she asked, "Why?" as if she sincerely couldn't understand the reason he was determined to ignore the chemistry between them.

He wasn't sure that he understood it, either, but he knew that it was necessary. "Because I don't even know how long I'm going to be in Rust Creek Falls, but I know it's not going to be forever," he reminded her.

"I'm not looking for a ring on my finger," she told him.

He lifted his brows, silently challenging the veracity of her claim, and her cheeks flushed again.

"Sure, I want to get married someday," she acknowledged, perhaps a little defensively. "But I didn't kiss you because I want to spend the rest of my life with you."

"Why did you kiss me?" he asked, though he suspected the answer could lead down a path he didn't want to follow.

She shrugged. "It seemed like a good idea at the time. But you don't have to worry," she hastened to assure him. "I'm not in the habit of throwing myself at men who don't want me."

It would be easy to let her believe that was true. That they'd shared a kiss, and the kiss hadn't done anything for him. But after the passionate embrace they'd shared, how could she possibly think he didn't want her?

He'd practically pounced on her like a starving man at a buffet, and that first taste had failed to sate him. Even now, a primitive hunger continued to gnaw at his belly. Of course, admitting that truth might be more dangerous than allowing her to believe a lie. But he knew it hurt to be rejected, and the last thing he wanted to do was hurt her—which was why he needed to keep a safe and careful distance from the appealingly sweet Eva Armstrong.

"If you believe I don't want you, then you haven't been paying attention," he chided gently.

A spark of something flared in those beautiful blue eyes and the corners of her mouth tipped up, just a little. "You do want me?"

Only more than he wanted to draw his next breath, but there was no way in hell he would admit it—especially when he couldn't do anything about it.

"I know you're planning to go back to Wyoming in a few weeks," she assured him. "I just don't understand why, if we enjoy spending time together, we can't occasionally hang out while you're here."

Though he was still wary, it seemed like a reasonable compromise. "I guess there's no harm in that," he said cautiously. "So long as you understand that there won't be any more kissing."

"Growing up with three sisters should have taught you that telling a woman she can't do something is a surefire way to make her try," she warned.

"It wasn't a challenge, Eva," he assured her.

"Okay," she said agreeably.

But there was a twinkle in her eye that warned Luke she had taken it as such. And he suspected that keeping his hands off the pretty baker was going to be more of a challenge than he could handle. More than he wanted to handle.

Because despite his assertion that it shouldn't happen again, now that he'd kissed her once, he wanted to do it over and over. He wanted to savor her intoxicating flavor; he wanted to feel the yield of those sweet lips; he wanted to revel in the press of her soft, feminine curves against his hard, aching body.

Yeah, he wanted all kinds of things he had no business wanting. "Good night, Eva."

"Good night, Luke."

Bella and Hudson were still out when Luke got back to their place, so he put the bowl of trifle in the refrigerator and settled himself on the sofa in front of the television. Scrolling through the channels, he found highlights of recent football games, but the replays on the screen failed to hold his attention. Instead, he was thinking about a certain sexy baker and the kiss that never should have happened.

Luke was generally pretty good at reading people, and it wasn't often someone said or did anything that surprised him. But when Eva moved in and kissed him, the bold action had caught him off guard.

It shouldn't have, because she'd given him fair warning. She'd outright told him that she was going to kiss him, so it wasn't really the move that surprised him so much as his own response to the overture.

He'd kissed her back, because while he still believed that getting romantically involved with anyone in Rust Creek Falls was a bad idea, he wasn't going to refuse the sweet offering. And because he couldn't help himself.

Because that first taste of her lips had made him want more.

A lot more.

"I didn't expect that you'd be home already."

The sound of his sister's voice jerked him back to the present.

"What?" He pressed the mute button on the remote so that he could focus on what she was saying. Not that he'd actually been watching the sports update, but he'd wanted to at least preserve the illusion that he was doing something other than thinking about Eva Rose Armstrong and the delicious flavor of her kiss.

"I said that I didn't expect you'd be home already," Bella repeated.

"It doesn't take a lot of time to eat a meal."

"Maybe not." She dropped onto the opposite end of the sofa, with her back against the arm so that she was facing him. "But I thought you might linger over coffee and dessert—because I know Eva would have made something fabulous for dessert or—" she drew the word out, then let it hang for a moment "—the good-night kiss."

He refused to let his sister goad him into saying anything about the kiss that he was desperately trying not to think about.

"Trifle," he said instead. "And yes, it was fabulous."

"And the kiss?" she prompted.

"Bella," he said, his tone admonishing.

"Oh, come on," she said, refusing to be admonished. "You can't expect me to believe that you shared a romantic dinner with a beautiful woman then went on your way without even a kiss good-night."

"It was a *friendly* dinner."

She rolled her eyes at that. "A woman doesn't usually offer to cook for a man because she wants to be friends."

"Eva knows that I'm not looking for any kind of relationship."

"So there was no wine? No candlelight?"

"No candlelight," he confirmed.

"No kiss?"

He ignored her question to ask his own instead. "How was your dinner?"

The speculative gleam in her eye warned that she was

aware of his redirection—and his refusal to deny that there was a kiss—but she seemed willing to let it slide, at least for now.

"Spectacular," she said. "We had chateaubriand with a peppercorn glaze, roasted new potatoes, sautéed julienned vegetables and the most amazing caramel pecan cheesecake for dessert."

"Good," he said. "If you've already had dessert, then you won't expect me to share my trifle."

"You didn't say what kind of trifle," she noted.

"*My* trifle," he said again.

Bella laughed softly. "Okay, *your* trifle."

"Where's Hudson?" he asked, because his sister's husband never seemed to be too far away from her when he was home.

"Not digging into your trifle," she promised. "He's in the office—he had some calls to make."

"At—" Luke glanced at the clock "—ten thirty-seven p.m.?"

"It's already tomorrow afternoon in Sydney."

"He works hard, doesn't he?"

"Harder than his brother ever gave him credit for," she said. "But he plays hard, too. He believes balance is important."

"Smart man."

Bella offered him a cheeky smile. "Smart enough to marry me anyway."

"Smart *and* lucky," he noted.

"Actually, I'm the lucky one," she said. "After everything that happened in the past, I never thought I'd find anyone who would love me. And I never dreamed that someone could love me the way that he does."

It was possible that nothing would have been different for Bella if he'd stayed, but that didn't prevent Luke from wishing he'd made different choices twelve years earlier. Not just after the funeral, but before their parents were killed.

"Have you ever been in love?"

He blinked, caught off guard—again—by the abrupt shift in the conversation. "Where did that come from?"

She shrugged. "You've been gone for almost twelve years—I'm curious about where you've been, what you've been doing, who you've been with."

"I've been in Wyoming," he reminded her. "Working on various ranches here and there."

"Who you've been with," she said again.

"I've dated some, had a few relationships, nothing serious."

"Not yet," she teased.

But he suspected the issue was something more than timing. "I'm not sure I'm capable of falling in love," he confided.

"Why would you say something like that?" she asked.

"I'm thirty-three years old," he reminded her. "If it was going to happen, don't you think it would have happened by now?"

"Not necessarily," she argued. "Maybe your heart needed a chance to finish grieving before it could start loving again."

He frowned at that.

"I was so hurt when you left," she admitted. "I didn't think about the fact that you were hurting, too."

"It was a long time ago."

She nodded. "But I still remember the emptiness I felt inside when you and Bailey and Danny disappeared from my life. I didn't think anything could be worse than losing Mom and Dad, but then I lost three of my brothers, too. And, only a few weeks later, both of my sisters."

"At least you and Jamie got to stay together," he said, because he had nothing else to offer. She'd been dealt a crappy hand—there was no disputing that fact.

"I would have been so lost without him," Bella said softly. "And then, when he went away to school, I really was lost—desperate for attention and affection. And I found it…in all the wrong places."

"What are you talking about?" he asked uneasily.

"I got pregnant, Luke."

Pregnant?

He was certain his jaw had dropped, but even when he closed it again, he couldn't find any words.

"I was fifteen—still a kid myself and facing the prospect of having a kid," she told him.

"Did you…have the baby?"

She shook her head. "I miscarried in the first trimester, but not before I'd told the grandparents about my pregnancy. A few months after my baby died, Grandma died, too, and Gramps blamed me."

"Oh, Bella, I'm so sorry."

"It wasn't your fault."

But it was. He'd abandoned his siblings. Yeah, he'd thought it was the right thing to do at the time—the only thing he could do. Discovering what had happened after that, how his family had fallen apart and scattered, he couldn't help but wish he'd made different choices.

"I wish I'd been here for you," he said.

"You're here now," she said.

"You're too forgiving."

"I carried a lot of hurt and anger for a lot of years,"

she admitted. "But it wasn't your fault. None of what happened was your fault."

"Ah, Bella, you were twelve years old." He scrubbed his hands over his face. "What do you remember about what happened?"

"More than you would think," she told him.

But she couldn't remember what she'd never known—that he was responsible for tearing their family apart.

The long pause across the telephone line had Eva wishing she'd ignored the instinct to share the excitement of her evening with her sister. But when she'd watched the lights of Luke's truck disappear down the road, she'd been bursting to tell someone about the kiss they'd shared. And the someone who was her usual confidante was also her sister and best friend.

Delphine was five years older than Eva—and infinitely wiser. Married for nine years to the man she'd fallen head over heels in love with in her first year at college and the mother of three adorable boys, Del was living Eva's dream.

Of course, Eva hadn't been at college long enough to fall in love. She'd decided to take her first year to focus on her studies, adjust to living away from home and being independent, and then her father's diagnosis had prevented her from returning for a second year.

She had no regrets about the choices she'd made, but she did sometimes wonder if changing course had completely derailed all her dreams. But tonight, after dinner with Luke, she was confident that her life would soon be back on track again.

Her sister was much less optimistic.

"Honey, when a guy says that he doesn't want to get

involved, you'd be smart to listen to him," Del said to her now. "Ignoring that kind of blatant warning is a tried-and-true recipe for heartache."

"I know you're right," she acknowledged.

"So why do I get the feeling that you're not going to heed my advice?"

She didn't deny it. "Because despite what he said, the way he kissed me—" Eva couldn't help but sigh, because her lips were still tingling and her blood still humming with the aftereffects of that incredibly delicious lip-lock. "I've never been kissed like that before."

"I'm sure it was a fabulous kiss," her sister said kindly. "But you can't spin dreams of a future on the basis of a single kiss."

"He's the one, Del. I know it."

"And a few months ago, Zach Dalton was the one. You were certain of it then, too."

Another truth she couldn't deny. Because Zach had been honest and up-front about what he wanted, and when he described his perfect woman, Eva met all of his criteria. Unfortunately, his heart wasn't in sync with his head, and he'd fallen in love with Lydia Grant instead.

"This time is different," she insisted.

Del's silence spoke volumes. She didn't need to point out that Eva had said those words before, too. Not just about Zach, but about Bobby Ray before Zach, and Jason before Bobby Ray. But the truth was, as much as Eva had wanted each of those men to be "the one" at the time she was with them, none of them had made her feel the way she felt when she was with Luke.

"You have such a warm and generous heart," Del finally said. "But if you keep giving pieces of it away, you're not going to have anything left for the man who truly does love you."

"How long am I supposed to wait for him?" Eva asked, not bothering to hide her frustration. "You were already married to Harrison for four years by the time you were my age."

"Love doesn't happen on any particular schedule, but when the right man comes along, you'll know it," Del promised.

But Luke *was* the right man, and Eva *did* know it.

She also knew better than to say so to her sister when Delphine was only trying to protect her from herself.

"In the meantime," she said instead, "is there any harm in spending time with a handsome cowboy?"

"That depends on whether you can spend time with him without falling in love," her sister cautioned.

"I can kiss a guy without expecting it to lead to a ring on my finger," she insisted.

"Without expecting it maybe," Del acknowledged. "But I don't think you can stop yourself from hoping for it."

"It's hard being single when everyone else I know is falling in love," she confided.

"Not everyone," her sister denied. "Amy is still single, and she's older than you."

In fact, Amy Wainwright was the same age as Delphine and, when they were growing up, she'd spent so much time at the Armstrong house that Eva had sometimes felt as if she had three sisters. Eva had always liked and admired her sister's friend, who was pretty and smart and seemed to excel at everything she did.

"How is Amy?" Eva asked now. "She hasn't been back to Rust Creek Falls for a long time."

Del sighed. "She's busy—too busy to make the trip home."

"And probably too busy to worry about pairing off," Eva guessed.

"Speaking of pears, with an e-a-r-s," her sister said in a deliberate effort to shift the topic of their conversation. "Harrison's mom gave me a recipe for cranberry sauce with plums that I was thinking I'd make for Christmas dinner."

"What's the connection between pears and plums?" she wondered aloud.

"They both grow on trees."

Eva laughed, her mood immediately lighter. "Well, don't tell Dad about the plums. You know he's particular about his cranberry sauce."

"I know," Del confirmed.

They talked for a while longer about the upcoming holiday.

Her sister confided that the kids' wish lists to Santa had been getting longer and longer every day until their parents had instructed them to pare—"p-a-r-e," Del clarified—them down to three things.

As Eva listened to her sister and laughed over her nephews' antics, she knew there was only one thing she wanted to find under the tree on Christmas morning: Luke Stockton.

Paper and bow optional.

Chapter Eight

Despite tossing and turning for a long time the previous night, Luke was up before the sun on Wednesday. Years of early morning responsibilities had created an internal alarm that invariably woke him before his clock ever did. And although he was technically on vacation and there was nowhere he had to be this morning, he resisted the urge to pull the covers over his head and go back to sleep, because slumber failed to provide any escape from the grief and guilt that continued to plague him.

He'd anticipated that being back in Rust Creek Falls would force him to confront the demons of his past. What he hadn't anticipated was his preoccupation with a certain sexy baker who, although not part of his past, kept slipping into his dreams. Tempting and teasing him.

He'd meant what he'd said to his sister the night before—he didn't know if he was capable of falling in love. He did know that he wasn't bothered by the prospect of spending his life alone. In fact, he preferred it that way.

Sure, he'd enjoyed spending time with Eva. She was good company and a definite pleasure to look at. And as delicious as her culinary creations were, her pies—and even her trifle—didn't begin to compare to the intoxicating flavor of her lips.

Everything about her was a feast for the senses. She smelled good—a temptingly sweet combination of vanilla and sugar—and she felt even better when she was in his arms. She was slender but with curves in all the right places, and even now his blood rushed hotly through his veins at the memory of those sweet curves pressed against him.

Muttering a curse under his breath, he shoved back the covers and headed into the bathroom for a shower.

A very cold shower.

"You're up early," Hudson noted when Luke wandered down to the kitchen a short while later.

"Old habits," he said. "What's your excuse?"

"Conference call with London."

He nodded. "Not so early in the UK."

"The joys of doing business in other time zones," Hudson noted, refilling his mug with coffee, then pouring another cup for his brother-in-law.

"Thanks."

Hudson nodded. "So what are your plans today?"

"I thought I might head over to Jamie's ranch, give him a hand with the morning chores."

"Mucking out stalls your idea of a good time?"

He shook his head. "Just another old habit."

"No doubt your brother could use the help. Whether or not he'll accept it is a whole other issue," Hudson warned.

Luke mulled over those words as he drove out to the Short Hills Ranch.

Jamie had always been determined to prove himself to his big brothers—eager to do everything they did and angry whenever they left him behind. And while Luke wanted to believe that Jamie's apparent refusal to accept help was just another example of this, he suspected that his youngest brother's stubbornness was rooted in something else. After Luke, Bailey and Danny left, Jamie had been forced to do everything on his own because there was no one around to help him.

With that thought weighing heavily on his mind, he stepped out of his truck. His boots crunched in the snow as he made his way toward the barn. Another set of prints led from the house to the same place, suggesting that his brother was already inside.

The Short Hills Ranch wasn't half as big as some of the spreads he'd worked in Wyoming. On the other hand, Jamie managed all the responsibilities of this land mostly on his own, with only occasional help from a neighbor's kid. Luke had surveyed the property on his first visit, and though everything had been—and still was—covered in snow, he'd noted that the perimeter fence was in good repair and the barn sported a new roof and recent paint. The horses were in the paddock now, wearing light blankets as added protection against the frigid temperatures, which suggested to Luke that his brother was likely mucking out their stalls.

He muscled open the heavy door, then stepped inside and closed it quickly behind him again so the heat wouldn't escape. He walked down the center aisle, breathing in the scents of fresh hay and old leather. The familiar and welcoming fragrance helped ease some of the knots in his belly.

"What are you doing here?" Jamie asked, the sharp edge in his voice tightening those knots again.

"I thought I could lend a hand around here while I'm in town," Luke offered.

His brother continued to mix fresh bedding with the unsoiled straw that he'd tossed aside while he cleaned out the stall. "You think a few hours' labor will make me forget that you abandoned us twelve years ago?" Jamie challenged.

"No," Luke said, his tone heavy with guilt and regret. "I just figured that I'm a ranch hand without work right now, and you've got a ranch that could use an extra hand."

"I manage okay."

"You've done more than manage okay," he said. "You've succeeded in building up a herd and providing for your family."

Jamie finished spreading the straw so that it covered the floor, then stepped out of the stall and turned to look at his brother. "You gonna stand there talking all day or muck out some stalls?"

"I'm gonna muck out some stalls," Luke told him.

Jamie nodded and let him get to work.

Luke had only been in Rust Creek Falls for a week but, in that time, he'd missed the physical labor that ranching entailed. Within a few hours, however, his unused muscles were feeling the effects of exertion. When he dumped the last of the soiled bedding, he was more than ready to be done.

He returned the wheelbarrow and shovel to the barn just as Jamie was coming out of his office.

"I appreciate the help," his brother said only a little begrudgingly. "Especially since I promised Danny that I'd squeeze out some time to give him a hand at Sunshine Farm this afternoon."

"I'm heading over there myself in a little while," Luke

told him, having promised the groom-to-be the same thing.

"Well, you might as well come in for lunch first," Jamie said. "You've earned a meal."

Luke had planned to head into town and grab a bite at Daisy's Donut Shop. Not that he was deliberately trying to cross paths with Eva, but he did have the empty trifle bowl in his truck to return to her. The unexpected offer from his brother, though, was one that he couldn't refuse.

Three days after she'd cooked dinner for Luke—three days after he'd kissed her until her head was spinning so that she could barely remember her own name—Eva acknowledged that maybe her sister was right to be worried.

She was aware that she had a tendency to fall hard and fast and, as a result, she'd had her heart broken more times than she wanted to count. But after the kiss they'd shared, she'd let herself believe that he wouldn't break her heart. That this time, she wouldn't be the only one to fall—and she wouldn't end up alone.

But after three days with only a few words exchanged between them when he came into Daisy's to grab a cup of coffee to go—and once to return the bowl he'd taken home with the leftover trifle—she'd started to doubt her own convictions. And then finally, late on Saturday afternoon, Luke stopped by the donut shop and settled into an empty seat at the counter.

"This is a surprise," Eva said.

"I thought I should get out for a while and give the newlyweds some space."

"I'd guess that they have plenty of space in that big house."

"They do," he agreed. "But I'm sure they're aware

that they aren't alone, so I told them I was going to be out for a few hours."

"And what do you plan on doing for those few hours?"

"That depends on you," he told her.

"Me?" she asked, pleased and surprised that he'd sought her out.

"Do you have any plans tonight?"

"None," she said quickly.

Maybe too quickly.

Did she sound too eager? Too desperate?

Maybe she should have pretended to have a social life—or at least feigned the possibility by checking the calendar on her phone.

But she had no plans—no social life at all, in fact. And if Luke wanted to spend time with her, then she was more than happy to do so.

"What did you have in mind?"

"A flyer posted on the community board at Crawford's advertised *Elf* as tonight's feature movie at the high school," he told her.

"Who doesn't love Will Ferrell?"

He smiled. "Is that a yes?"

"If you're asking if I want to go with you…sure," she decided.

He nodded. "The movie starts at eight—what time do you finish here?"

"I'm not actually working," Eva said, untying the apron she'd wrapped around her waist to protect her clothes while she was in the kitchen. "I just came in to assemble and decorate the cake for a seventy-fifth birthday."

"Then why don't we make it dinner and a movie?" he suggested.

Dinner and a movie sounded a lot like a date to Eva, and she felt a giddy rush of anticipation through her veins. But she knew that Luke was wary about any romantic involvement, and just because it sounded like a date to her didn't mean that it was a date to him, so she tried to play it cool.

"We've got meatloaf with mushroom gravy and mashed potatoes on the menu tonight," she told him.

He shook his head. "I had something else in mind."

She frowned at his quick response. "You don't like meatloaf?"

"I don't think you'd be able to sit here and enjoy a meal without rushing into the kitchen to check on one thing or another," he said.

"You've been away for a lot of years," she reminded him. "Perhaps you've forgotten that there aren't a lot of dining options in this town."

"I haven't forgotten," he assured her. "In fact, I've been craving a bacon cheeseburger from the Ace in the Hole since I passed the 'Welcome to Rust Creek Falls' sign."

"They do make a good burger," she acknowledged. And although the local bar and grill was a little rough around the edges and frequently the site of fisticuffs between cowboys who liked to work hard and party harder, the food was usually decent and the beer was always cold.

"I know the crowd there can get a little rowdy on weekends," he noted, anticipating her objection. "But we should be in and out before any of the local ranch hands get too drunk and stupid."

"I'm not worried," she said. "But I do want to go home to freshen up and change my clothes first."

His gaze skimmed over her from the top of her head

to the toes of her cowboy boots and back again. The slow appraisal made her skin tingle and her heart pound. Then he spoke—

"Why?" he asked. "You look fine to me."

—and the bubble burst.

"Because I'm a girl," she said with just a hint of exasperation in her voice. "And I'd like to elevate my appearance to something more than *fine*."

"What's wrong with fine?" he asked, clearly baffled by her response.

She just shook her head. "Fine is—" she searched for an explanation that would make sense to him. "It's the equivalent of satisfactory or adequate."

"You'd rather be unsatisfactory or inadequate?"

"I'd rather look nice," she told him. "Maybe even pretty."

His brows drew together. "Why would you aim for nice or pretty when you're already beautiful?"

His matter-of-fact tone stunned her as much as his words. "If you think I'm beautiful, why did you say I looked fine?" she demanded, full-on exasperation in her tone now.

"Because I figured you didn't need to be told and I didn't want you to worry that I was hitting on you."

She only *wished* he was hitting on her, but he'd been clear that wasn't going to happen—which didn't mean she couldn't attempt to change his mind.

"I'd still like to change before we go out," she told him.

Luke shrugged. "How much time do you need?"

"I'll be ready in half an hour."

And she would use every one of those thirty minutes to ensure that when he looked at her, he wouldn't be thinking that she looked *fine*.

* * *

There were a lot of reasons that Eva loved her job at Daisy's—one of which was the proximity of the donut shop to her parents' house. Less than five minutes after she left Luke sitting with his coffee, she was climbing the steps to the front porch of her childhood home.

She was surprised that her dad's SUV wasn't in the driveway, which meant that one or both of her parents was out. If it was both, she would be saved from having to explain her own plans. Marion was already worried about the time Eva was spending with Luke, and she didn't want maternal concern to put a damper on her excitement about the evening ahead.

She'd just opened the door when her cell phone chimed to indicate a text message.

Gone out for dinner. There's leftover chicken and rice in the fridge if you want it.

Love Mom & Dad

Eva keyed in her reply:

OK. I'm going to the movie at the high school tonight. See you later. XO

Then she hurried upstairs to survey the contents of her closet, trying to decide what to wear for a date that wasn't really a date.

She didn't usually bother with much makeup because the heat from the ovens caused it to melt off her face. Since she didn't have to worry about that tonight, she darkened her lashes with mascara, colored her cheeks with powder and slicked her lips with gloss. Then she unbraided her hair and brushed it out so it hung in loose waves to her shoulders. She wrinkled her nose at the reflection in the mirror, glanced at the time and plugged in her straightening iron.

While the appliance was heating, she stripped out of her clothes and rifled through her closet, looking for her favorite wrap-style skirt. It was navy with tiny flowers embroidered all over it, and it paired nicely with the slim-fitting V-neck cashmere top in the same pale shade of blue as the flowers. She found what she was looking for and tossed both garments on top of her bed while she wriggled into a pair of wool tights. They weren't sexy but they were necessary in December, and they wouldn't be visible beneath the long skirt anyway.

After dressing, she straightened her hair, then added hoop earrings, a trio of bangle bracelets and a teardrop-style pendant on a long chain that hung between her breasts. Maybe it wasn't very subtle, but if Luke still intended to leave town after the holidays, she didn't have time for subtlety. A light spritz of perfume and she was ready to go.

And just in time, she realized, as the doorbell chimed.

She stuffed her feet into her boots, grabbed her jacket from the hook and opened the door.

Luke had decided to hang out at Daisy's for the half hour Eva had said she needed, though he was skeptical of that claim. If she could truly be ready in thirty minutes, she was more efficient than any other woman he'd ever dated.

Not that this was a date—not really. He'd left his sister's house with the intention of grabbing a bite and catching a movie, and since he enjoyed Eva's company, he'd asked her to join him. And even if a man and woman sharing a meal and enjoying entertainment together might technically fit the definition of a date, he'd made it clear to Eva that he wasn't looking to get involved.

But that was before she opened the door in response to his knock and he discovered that she had, indeed, elevated her appearance from beautiful to breathtaking.

His gaze skimmed over her, from the top of her head to the toes of her boots and back again. The heat in his eyes as they made their slow perusal warmed every part of her—including some parts that had been cold for a very long time.

"You look like champagne and caviar, not beer and burgers," he told her.

Eva ignored the way her heart was bumping against her ribs and replied lightly, "I'm flattered you think so, but my champagne and caviar outfit is at the dry cleaners."

"I didn't think Rust Creek Falls had a dry cleaner."

"It doesn't," she said. "I had to take it into Kalispell."

He chuckled as he offered his arm and led her to his truck.

It was a testament to the quality of the food even more than the limited dining options in Rust Creek Falls that the Ace was always packed on Friday and Saturday nights. Luke took her hand to help her up the rough-hewn wooden steps, then opened the door beneath the oversize ace of hearts playing card that blinked in red neon. They stepped inside the dimly lit bar just as a waitress moved past with a tray full of drinks.

"Grab a seat anywhere," she told them. "If you can find one."

Luke took a moment to glance around, then steered her toward a booth that had just been vacated, staking claim to it while the busboy was still clearing away the dirty dishes.

"Do you know what you want or do you need to look at a menu?" he asked as the waitress approached.

Though what she really wanted wasn't something she would find on the menu, Eva smiled at the server and said, "I'll have the bacon cheeseburger."

"With fries?"

"Sure," she agreed, because no one went to the Ace for a salad.

"Anything to drink?"

"Diet cola."

The waitress jotted the order down on her pad then turned to Luke.

"I'll have the same," he said. "But real cola."

After she'd gone, Luke leaned back in his seat and looked around the room. "Does that ancient Wurlitzer still work?"

"It does," Eva confirmed. "And it still plays three songs for a quarter."

"What's with the giant-screen TV on the stage?"

"Rosey had that brought in so her customers can watch *The Great Roundup* on Friday nights."

"People actually come to a bar to watch a reality show?" he asked.

"They do," she confirmed. "Because Rust Creek Falls has two residents—Travis Dalton and Brenna O'Reilly—competing for the prize money and, of course, we're all rooting for one of them to win."

"Yeah, my sister told me." But he still looked skeptical.

"You should be here on a Friday night," she told him. "It's standing room only. Once I heard a customer grumble about the number of people packed into the place, but his threat to report the establishment to the fire chief was overheard by the fire chief, who promised to look into the situation as soon as the final credits rolled."

Luke chuckled at that, then did a double take. "Wow— there's a man over there who looks just like my high school history teacher."

Eva didn't need to follow the direction of his gaze. "Did you have Mr. Armstrong for history?"

He nodded. "You, too?"

"No, but I know him very well. He's actually the principal of the high school now. And my father."

Chapter Nine

Eva held her breath as she waited for Luke to respond to her confession.

"That would explain the glare," he noted.

"He's not really glaring," she hastened to assure him. "He's just trying to figure out who you are because he's not wearing his glasses."

Luke shook his head. "I can't believe I didn't make the connection between Eva Armstrong and Mr. Armstrong in the history department."

"Armstrong isn't an uncommon name," she said. "And a lot of people try to forget about high school history."

"It wasn't so bad," he said.

She just lifted a brow, making him laugh.

"Okay, it was awful," he admitted. "But the truth is, I didn't enjoy any of my subjects because the whole time that I was stuck inside a classroom, I only wanted to be helping my dad out on the ranch."

"A cowboy through and through," she noted.

"I guess so," he acknowledged.

Thankfully, her parents had finished their meals and, after they'd paid their check, stood up to leave. But of course, they didn't go without stopping by their daughter's table first.

Luke automatically rose to his feet.

Ray Armstrong shook his hand. "Luke Stockton—I heard that you were back in town. From Wyoming?"

Luke confirmed with a nod.

"You plan on moving back to Rust Creek Falls?" his former teacher asked.

"No, sir. Just visiting for a while."

"Obviously you know my dad," Eva said, eager to cut off her father's interrogation. "And this is my mom, Marion."

Luke inclined his head. "It's a pleasure to meet you, ma'am."

"And it's nice to finally put a face to the name Eva has been—"

"Your message didn't say where you'd gone for dinner," Eva interjected before her mother could complete her sentence.

"I was hoping to talk your father into going somewhere else," Marion confided. "He knows this isn't one of my favorite places."

"But nowhere else does a burger like the Ace," Ray pointed out.

"Actually, the burgers you cook on the backyard grill are even better," his wife noted.

"The backyard grill that's currently under eighteen inches of snow?"

Marion sighed. "Which is why we're here."

"But now we're going," Ray said, and Eva sent him a quick smile of thanks.

Her father didn't smile back, and Eva suspected that

he would be watching the clock as he waited for her to return home after the movie.

"Was that as uncomfortable for you as it was for me?" she asked Luke when her parents had gone.

"Actually, it wasn't as uncomfortable as I'd feared," he said.

"At least that brief conversation confirmed that I hit the jackpot with their Christmas present," she noted.

"What did you get them?" Luke asked after the waitress had delivered their drinks.

"An indoor grill."

He studied her across the table. "Did you know that you get a sparkle in your eye whenever you talk about the holidays?"

"I love Christmas," she said simply.

He picked up his glass and sipped.

"And you don't," she guessed, feeling disappointed for him that he wasn't looking forward to the holiday.

"I don't dislike it," he denied. "I just don't get all excited about it, like…"

"Like a kid at Christmas?" she finished for him.

The corner of his mouth turned up in a half smile. "Yeah, like that."

"Why not?"

He shrugged. "I have a lot of happy memories of Christmases from my childhood, but when my parents died, everything changed."

She touched a hand to his arm. "I'm sorry."

"It was a long time ago," he said.

She knew it was true, but she also knew that he was still feeling raw. Twelve years had passed since he'd left Rust Creek Falls, but coming home now, for the first time, it was understandable that all of the memories—good and bad—would come back to him in a flood.

"And I know I promised to stay in town for Danny and Annie's wedding, but I have reservations about being here Christmas morning," he confided.

"Why's that?"

"Because Bella and Hudson are still newlyweds and I'm sure they'd prefer to spend their first Christmas together alone."

"And I'm sure that, after twelve years, there's nothing your sister wants more than to celebrate the holidays with her family—her whole family," Eva pointed out to him.

"Except that the whole family won't be together," he pointed out.

Eva knew that Hudson's investigator hadn't yet managed to track down Bailey or Liza, but she suspected that he wasn't referring to a sibling reunion, but the loss of his parents.

"Tell me how you spend your Christmas morning," he suggested, as if to distract from his own thoughts and memories.

"With my parents and sisters and their husbands and kids. We gather around the tree early—because the kids don't let us sleep past six—and we drink hot cider or Irish coffee, nibble on fresh fruit and sticky buns and open presents."

"Your sisters come home every Christmas?"

"Every Christmas," she confirmed. "Calla and Patrick will celebrate with his family in Thunder Canyon on Christmas Eve before they come here. Delphine's in-laws retired to Arizona a couple years back, so they usually head south on the twenty-sixth."

"Do you have a big meal later?"

She nodded. "A huge roast turkey with all of the trimmings."

"And pie for dessert?" he guessed.

"Pie for dessert," she confirmed.

"Apple?"

She chuckled. "Apple and lemon and pumpkin."

"I thought pumpkin pie was a Thanksgiving tradition."

"Not exclusively," she said. "And I thought apple was your favorite."

"It is," he acknowledged. "But I've recently discovered that I have more of a sweet tooth than I ever knew."

But he declined the offer of dessert when the waitress came around to clear away their empty plates, expressing a desire to save room for popcorn at the movie.

The high school was only a couple blocks from the Ace—a pleasant walk in the warmer months but an inadvisable one in December, so after settling their bill, they drove over. Tickets were sold at a table set up in the main foyer and only cash payment was accepted. Eva knew to ensure that she had small bills whenever she attended because it wasn't unusual for the cash box to be short on change.

Tonight Luke paid for their admission, then led the way to the concession area and joined the end of the line.

"Popcorn?" he offered.

"I couldn't even finish the fries that came with my burger," she reminded him.

"I'm guessing that's a no?"

"That's a no," she confirmed.

"Soda?"

"No, thanks."

Eva shook her head as he came away with a large bag

of popcorn and a cola in hand. "You can't honestly still be hungry."

"It has nothing to do with hunger and everything to do with enhancing the movie-watching experience," he told her.

"I'll take your word for it," she said dubiously.

There was a pretty good crowd gathered tonight. Of course, there weren't a lot of entertainment options in town, and the high school gym was a favorite weekend destination for those who didn't want to hang with the sometimes rowdy crowd at the Ace.

Eva and Luke found seats near the back of the gymnasium, leaving the rows closer to the front for families with children. There weren't any previews or commercials—the only warning that the movie was about to start, apart from the lights being switched off, was Mr. Hendricks—the caretaker—standing at the front of the room and shouting out a reminder for everyone to turn off their cell phones.

Elf was one of Eva's favorite Christmas movies, but about halfway through, she realized that she hadn't been paying attention to the feature. But how was she supposed to concentrate on the screen when the man beside her was so distracting? Especially when, every time Luke leaned close to say something to her, his breath tickled her ear and sent shivers down her spine. And despite her insistence that she didn't want any popcorn, he kept jiggling the bag in front of her, silently encouraging her to share. She finally succumbed to temptation—at least with respect to the popcorn. But it was the man she really wanted.

When the credits finally began to roll, she was grateful that she no longer had to pretend to be watching the movie but also disappointed that her time with Luke was coming to an end.

Maybe he was disappointed, too, because after helping with her coat, he said, "How does hot chocolate and a jelly donut sound?"

"The sound would be my stomach exploding," she told him.

"Just hot chocolate?" he suggested as an alternative.

"If you want hot chocolate, we can go for hot chocolate," she agreed.

"I'm not sure that I really want hot chocolate," he admitted. "But I am sure that I don't want to take you home yet."

"Oh," she said as happy butterflies swooped and twirled in her belly.

"I guess that wasn't very subtle, was it?"

"I prefer honesty to subtlety," she told him.

"Then it would be okay to admit that, every time I look at you, you take my breath away?"

"Well...that's a distinct improvement over 'you look fine,'" she noted.

He winced. "You must have realized by now that males have a tendency to fumble when they're in the company of a female they want to impress."

"Careful," she warned, "or I might start to think you're flirting with me."

"I shouldn't be," he admitted. "But I can't seem to help myself."

Her lips curved as he pushed open the door for her to exit, her smile widening even more when she stepped outside. "Look—it's snowing."

And it was—the sky was filled with great big fluffy

flakes that seemed to dance rather than fall in the dark night.

"Christmas snow," she said softly, reverently.

"What's Christmas snow?"

She threw her arms out to her sides, tipped her face up to the sky and turned in a slow circle. "This," she told him.

He held out a hand, watched a fat flake land on the palm of his leather glove and slowly melt away. "It looks like regular snow to me."

Eva shook her head. "Christmas snow is magic."

"Magic, huh?"

She nodded.

"And is this magic snow capable of creating some kind of enchantment?" he wondered aloud.

"Of course," she agreed.

"Is that why I suddenly find myself wanting to kiss you despite promising that it wouldn't happen again?"

"It might be the snow…or it might be that you're wildly attracted to me," she said.

Though her tone projected confidence, he could see the uncertainty in her eyes. But Luke, looking at her now—her cheeks pink from the cold, her eyes sparkling, her lips tipped up at the corners—wasn't uncertain at all.

"You might be right," he acknowledged.

She took a step toward him. "About the snow—or the attraction?"

His gaze lingered on the temptingly sweet curve of her mouth. "Either way, didn't we agree that any kind of romantic involvement would be a bad idea?"

"Who said anything about a romantic involvement?" she challenged. "Sometimes a kiss is just a kiss."

"Sometimes it is," he agreed just before his lips brushed against hers.

With a soft sigh, Eva's eyelids fluttered and her lips yielded. Luke's mouth was warm and firm and masterful, causing ribbons of desire to unfurl in her belly and spread slowly through her veins. His hands slid up her back, then down again. Even through the bulky coat she wore, she felt the heat of his touch, and she wanted more.

She lifted her arms to his shoulders, slid her hands into the silky ends of his hair and held on while the world spun around her. She felt the gentle brush of snowflakes on her face, but not even the biting wind could chill the heat in her veins.

His tongue skimmed across the seam of her lips, and they parted willingly, eagerly, so that he could deepen the kiss. She didn't know how long they stood there, in the shadows of the trees, under the falling snow. She lost complete track of time, all sense of purpose. There was only Luke and this moment. Nothing else mattered.

"I don't think that kiss was just a kiss," he said when he finally eased his mouth from hers and had given them each a moment to catch their breath.

But his arms stayed around her, holding her close, and she wondered if he could hear the pounding of her heart, or even feel it against his chest.

"What was it?" she asked, wanting to know what he was thinking and feeling, desperate for some hint that she wasn't the only one who was starting to fall.

"It felt to me like the start of something bigger," he admitted, but he didn't sound happy about it.

"And you don't want to start anything," she remembered.

"It wouldn't be fair to start something that I'm not going to be in town long enough to finish."

She knew that she should be grateful he'd put on the brakes, but it was difficult to be grateful when her body was still aching for more. And why was he so certain that anything they started had to finish? Was it really so impossible to believe that he might fall in love and want to build a life with her? But of course she didn't ask any of those questions.

"What about that hot chocolate?" she said instead. "Do you still want that?"

"If you're not in any hurry to get home," he said.

"Is my carriage going to turn into a pumpkin?"

He smiled. "It's not even close to midnight."

"Then I think I've got time."

Eva wasn't surprised to find that her mom was still up when Luke dropped her off. She was surprised that her dad wasn't in his recliner beside her, flipping through the channels on TV and grumbling that there was nothing worth watching while his wife knitted tiny hats and boo-ties and baby blankets for the Tree of Hope at Crawford's.

She settled on the opposite end of the sofa from her mother, tucking her feet under her skirt. "Where's Dad?"

Marion's needles clicked in a familiar rhythm. "In bed."

"Is everything okay?" Eva asked, immediately worried, because when someone you loved had battled cancer— even successfully—the worry never quite went away.

"Everything's fine," her mother hastened to reassure her. "But we had an early morning and a busy day, and we drew straws to determine who could go to bed and who should wait up until you got home."

"You don't usually wait up for me," she noted.

"No," her mother agreed. "But I wanted to know how your evening was."

"Good," she said cautiously.

"Luke seems like a nice man. He's certainly a handsome one."

"He is," she agreed.

"Has he said how long he's planning to stay in Rust Creek Falls?"

"At least until his brother's Christmas Eve wedding," Eva said.

"And then he's going back to Wyoming?"

"That seems to be the plan," she acknowledged.

"You know why I'm asking, don't you?" her mother asked.

"You want to know if you need to set another place at the table for dinner on Christmas?"

Marion sighed as she tugged on the yarn. "I'm worried about you."

"There's no reason for you to worry," Eva told her.

"You're falling in love with him."

"Maybe," she admitted.

Her mother continued to knit. After another minute she said, "And when he leaves, he's going to break your heart."

"Maybe," she said again.

She understood her mother's concerns; she knew they were valid. She did have a habit of giving her heart too quickly—and having it broken easily and frequently.

"Or maybe he'll fall in love with me, too, and decide to stay in Rust Creek Falls," she suggested as an alternative.

"Maybe he will," her mother acknowledged, though the doubtful tone warned Eva that she didn't believe it was a real possibility. "Has he told you why he and his brothers left town?"

She picked a piece of fluff off the arm of the sofa. "Not really."

"Maybe you should ask him," Marion suggested.

"I figure if he wanted me to know, he would tell me."

"But don't *you* want to know?"

Of course, she did. Especially if his reasons for leaving twelve years ago were unchanged, because then it was likely that he would be leaving again. But watching him with his family, she'd seen the longing in his eyes, and she knew that he wanted to stay, even if he wasn't ready to admit it to himself.

"It's not really any of my business," she finally said in response to her mother's question.

"It is if you're thinking of a future with this man."

"Right now, I'm just enjoying being with him."

Her mother set her knitting aside and reached over to rest a hand on Eva's knee. "You deserve to fall in love with a man who will love you as much as you love him," she said. "I'm just not sure that Luke Stockton is that man."

"You've got some pretty strong opinions about a man you just met tonight," she noted.

"You're right. But I'm less concerned about misjudging him than I am about him hurting you."

"Do you remember what you said to me before I went away to college?" Eva asked.

"Probably some brilliant words of wisdom that you're going to toss back in my face now," her mother guessed.

"You said that I shouldn't ever let fear of what might happen prevent me from following my heart."

Marion sighed. "It seemed like good advice at the time."

"It was," Eva agreed. "And it's the advice I'm going to follow now, too."

Chapter Ten

Bella had encouraged Luke to come and go as he pleased, reminding him that he had a key and the alarm code and didn't need to worry about what anyone else was doing. It had taken him a few days before he felt comfortable enough to do so, but until he pulled into the driveway and discovered the house illuminated by hundreds—no, thousands—of Christmas lights, he didn't realize that this was the first time he'd been out after dark.

He kicked off his boots and hung his coat in the closet, then headed toward the stairs and his guest room on the second level. As he approached the family room, he heard the murmur of voices from within. Obviously his sister and brother-in-law were still up—a realization that tempted him to tiptoe past the doorway because he knew that if Bella knew he'd been out with Eva, his sister would commence round two of her interrogation.

On the other hand, maybe he should solicit her opinion because he obviously didn't have a clue about what he was doing—telling Eva in one breath that he didn't want to get involved and then kissing her breathless in the next.

Eva had claimed that the snow was magic, but he suspected it was the woman herself who had cast some kind of spell on him. He'd been attracted to his share of women and had been fortunate that his feelings were usually reciprocated, but he couldn't ever remember being so captivated so quickly by anyone else.

"Luke—is that you?" Bella's voice called out.

"It's me," he confirmed, stepping through the doorway and into the room to find his sister snuggled in her husband's arms, her back to his front.

Flames crackled in the fireplace, and a bottle of wine was open on the table, two half-full glasses beside it. There were more holiday decorations in here, including an enormous tree that stretched floor to ceiling and was wrapped in lights, garland and decorated with baubles and balls.

"There are glasses in the hutch," Hudson said, nodding his head toward the dining room. "If you want a glass of wine."

Luke shook his head. "I'm not sure that would mix well with the hot chocolate I just had."

"You've been hanging out at Daisy's again," Bella guessed.

"Not hanging out," he denied. "But we did go there after the movie."

"We?" she prompted, a speculative gleam in her eyes.

"Me and Eva," he admitted.

"You've been spending a lot of time with her lately," his sister noted.

"Which is nobody's business but your own," Hudson said, surprising Luke with the unexpected defense.

"Is it wrong to want to know about the woman my brother's dating?" she challenged.

"We're not dating," Luke told her. "We've just been... hanging out."

"Is that all it is?"

He wanted to answer yes—firmly and definitively—but the taste of Eva still lingered on his lips; want for her still pulsed in his blood.

"Eva knows that I'm not in any position to get involved right now," he pointed out to his sister, and reminded himself.

"Why not?" she pressed, the expression on her face matching the disappointment in her tone.

"Because my life is in Wyoming," he reminded her.

"It doesn't have to be. You could come home, Luke, to be near your family again."

After less than two weeks in Rust Creek Falls, he was more tempted by her entreaty than he'd ever thought he would be. But his sister wouldn't want him to move back to Rust Creek Falls if she knew the truth about why he'd left. If she knew that he was responsible for tearing their family apart.

He'd always thought the self-imposed exile was his punishment for being responsible for the loss of their parents. He hadn't known that the deaths of Lauren and Rob were only the beginning. He'd chosen to walk away—confident that Jamie, Bella, Liza and Dana would be taken care of by their grandparents. He hadn't known that their family had been further torn apart, that Liza and Dana had been put up for adoption, that Jamie and Bella had been given a roof over their heads but not much more.

His heart ached for all of them, but for Bella most of all. He couldn't fathom everything she'd been through—a teenage pregnancy and miscarriage followed by the death of their grandmother. Yet, by some miracle of fate, she'd gotten through all of that. And looking at her now, snuggled in the loving arms of her husband, Luke was both grateful and relieved to know that she'd found a partner who loved and appreciated the wonderful woman she was.

Jamie had traveled an equally rocky path to get where he was, including the death of his first wife only hours after the birth of their three babies. But he had worked hard to make his ranch a success for himself and his children, and he'd even found love again with his longtime friend and confidante.

Danny had been miserable when he left Rust Creek Falls with Luke and Bailey, but he'd eventually found his way home again to reconnect with his high school sweetheart and discover that he was the father of an eleven-year-old daughter he never knew existed. And while Luke suspected their reunion had been more painful and complicated than he knew, they were now planning a wedding and future together.

He was sincerely happy for each of them, genuinely grateful that they'd managed—seemingly against all odds—to find happiness and contentment in their lives. Although he'd lost touch with Bailey years earlier when his brother had headed to New Mexico, he drew comfort from the knowledge that Bailey was with the woman he loved—likely married and possibly even a father now, too.

He didn't know anything about what his two youngest sisters had been doing for the past twelve years, but he was looking forward to seeing Dana at the wedding. According to Bella, their twenty-year-old sister had been adopted by a wonderful couple and raised in a loving home. He could only hope that Liza had fared as well—

and that Hudson's private investigator would track her and Bailey down soon so that their reunion might be as complete as possible.

"Luke?"

He looked down at the hand on his arm, then up into his sister's concerned face.

"Are you okay?" Bella asked gently.

"Sorry," he said. "My mind just wandered for a minute."

"And we should wander up to bed," Hudson suggested to his wife.

"All right," Bella agreed. Then to Luke, "He thinks if I pressure you, you're going to hightail it back to Wyoming, but I just want you to know how much I want you to stay."

"I do know, Bella," he said, sincerely touched by her entreaty.

"And you're thinking about it, right?"

"Bella," Hudson said, shaking his head.

"I'm thinking about it," he said, if only to appease her.

But after her husband had dragged her out of the room and he was alone with his thoughts, he was surprised to realize that it was true.

Sunday brunch had been a tradition in the Armstrong house for as long as Eva could remember, and it was the sound and scent of sizzling bacon that lured her downstairs the following morning.

Her father was already at the table, with a mug of coffee in one hand and the *Gazette* in the other.

"What can I do to help?" Eva asked, as she always did.

"Everything's under control," her mother said, as she always did.

So Eva poured herself a mug of coffee and took her usual seat at the table.

Ray finished with his paper, folded it in half and set it aside just as his wife carried a platter loaded with crisp bacon, creamy eggs and fluffy pancakes to the table.

"Breakfast looks almost as good as you," he said with a lascivious wink for his wife.

"Flattery won't get you out of helping with the cleanup," Marion told him.

It was another common exchange—a comfortable routine they'd established over the years. And though Ray would, predictably, grumble when his wife handed him a tea towel, he never actually balked at doing his share of kitchen duty.

Her parents were the reason why Eva had so much faith in the power of love. For all of her twenty-five years, they'd been an example to her, and it never failed to warm her heart to see that, after thirty-seven years of marriage, three kids and countless crises—the worst of which had been her father's bout with cancer five years before—they were still head over heels in love.

When she was a teenager, their overt displays of affection had sometimes made her squirm. Now that she was older, she could appreciate how fortunate they were to have found one another. As were each of her sisters.

That was what Eva wanted, too. A partner in life. Someone to stand with her through the good times and not-so-good times. Someone she could count on to always be there for her.

She wanted Luke Stockton to be that man. And maybe she did have a tendency to fall hard and fast, but when she was with Luke, she forgot about every other man she'd ever dated. When she was with Luke, she forgot about everything but how much she wanted to be with Luke—forever.

Maybe she was jumping the gun a little. After all, she'd known him for less than two weeks and they'd only shared two kisses. But she felt as if she'd known him a lot longer, and those kisses made her believe they were but a prelude to something more.

Her cell phone buzzed as she was nibbling on the last bite of her bacon. She glanced apologetically at her mother, conscious of the "no cell phones at the table" rule.

"Go ahead," Marion relented. "Everyone's finished eating."

Eva pushed away from the table to retrieve the device from the windowsill above the sink. She felt a flutter in her belly as she wondered if—and hoped that—it might be a message from Luke.

But it wasn't. It was her boss, asking if she could cover Karen's shift that afternoon. Eva hesitated. Although it was only a four-hour commitment, it would mean four fewer hours that she could spend with Luke.

On the other hand, Luke hadn't asked her to spend any time with him today. In fact, when he'd dropped her off the night before, he hadn't made any mention of when he might see her again. Besides, she'd had a life before he came to town and she would have a life again when he left. But she really hoped he would change his mind about going back to Wyoming and decide to stay in Rust Creek Falls instead.

In the meantime, Daisy had given her a job when she desperately needed one—not just for the income to help her parents out but to give her a reason to stay home during her dad's treatments. So she could text back only one reply:

Happy to help.

When Eva agreed to work Sunday afternoon, she'd resigned herself to the fact that she wouldn't see Luke that day. It was after four o'clock and halfway through her shift when the bell over the door jangled and he walked in.

"Hey," he said, obviously surprised to see her. "I thought you were supposed to be off all weekend."

Which confirmed, to her profound disappointment, that he hadn't come in looking for her but had another reason for being there. "I was—but Karen's in bed with the flu." She held up a mug, a silent question.

Luke glanced at his watch, then nodded and took a seat at the counter. "Have you ever said no when someone asks for a favor?"

"Of course I have," she responded.

"Really?" he challenged, accepting the mug she passed across the counter. "Tell me when."

"Well, I can't remember offhand," she admitted. "But I'm sure that I have."

"I'll bet you haven't," he said. "You're the type of person who just can't turn away from someone in need... which is kind of what I'm counting on."

She eyed him warily. "What do you mean?"

"I need help."

"What can I do?" she immediately offered.

Luke smiled. "See? You didn't even ask what—you just said yes."

"I said, 'what can I do?'" she clarified.

"And the answer is, help me with my Christmas shopping."

"I'd be happy to," she agreed. "I love shopping, especially this time of year when the stores are all decked out for the holidays."

"I was hoping you'd say that," he said. "But that's not actually why I'm here."

"So tell me why you are here," she suggested.

"I've been invited to dinner tonight and I realized, when I was at your door emptyhanded, that I probably shouldn't have shown up emptyhanded, so I offered to take something for dessert."

"Excuse me for a second," she said, grabbing the pot of coffee and moving to the other end of the counter to top up Homer Gilmore's cup.

Not because he'd asked for a refill, but because she needed an excuse to turn away so that Luke wouldn't see how much his casual admission of a date with another woman had hurt her.

And not only was he going on a date with another woman, but he'd come into Daisy's to pick up something for dessert—likely something Eva had made. It was just like Lydia Grant's request for lemon meringue pie all over again.

She chatted with the old man for a minute, until she was fairly confident that she could return to her conversation with Luke without crying. She set the pot back on the warmer and forced a smile. "We've got a small six-layer German chocolate cake that a customer ordered for his girlfriend's birthday before he found out she was allergic to nuts."

"I don't think nuts are a problem," he said.

She took the cake out of the case to show him.

"That looks yummy—and the perfect size for four people."

"A double date?"

"What?" He seemed sincerely baffled by the question, then he laughed. "No, it's not a date at all."

"It's not?"

"No," he said again. "I'm having dinner with Danny, Annie and Janie."

"Oh," she said, feeling foolish.

"Did you really think I would come in here to get dessert for a date with another woman?"

"Well, you admitted that you didn't expect to find me working today," she reminded him.

"I didn't," he confirmed. "But I was happy to see you."

She pulled a flat piece of cardboard out from under the counter and began forming a box for the cake.

"Is this the first time you're meeting your niece?" she asked, eager to change the topic of conversation and forget that she'd jumped to embarrassing and erroneous conclusions.

"It is," he confirmed.

"While you're having dinner tonight, you should listen for any hints about what Janie might want for Christmas," Eva suggested as she set the cake in the box and closed the lid. "Preteen girls are notoriously picky and it would be good to have a starting point before you go shopping."

"Before *we* go shopping," he reminded her.

She punched the price of his cake and coffee into the register, and he passed some bills across the counter. "When are we going shopping?"

"Whatever day works best for you."

"Wednesday?"

He picked up the cake box and winked at her. "It's a date."

Luke was glad he'd stopped by Daisy's Donut Shop to pick up something for dessert—not just because the cake scored big points for him with his niece and future sister-in-law, but also because talking to Eva helped him forget, at least momentarily, that he was nervous about the family dinner.

By the time Janie got up to clear the dessert dishes from the table, Luke was surprised to realize that they'd been sitting around the table for almost three hours. Even more surprising was how much he'd enjoyed the time he'd spent getting reacquainted with his brother's fiancée and finally meeting his niece. A few weeks earlier, he wouldn't have believed it was possible for love to endure through so many life events and so much time apart, but Danny and Annie proved him wrong.

After Janie excused herself to go do homework, Annie began the washing up. Danny and Luke offered to help, but she shooed them out of the kitchen.

"She doesn't seem like one of those bridezillas you hear horror stories about," Luke noted.

"Annie's not the type to sweat the small stuff," Danny agreed. "The only thing she was really worried about was the venue."

"And it's all ready to go."

His brother snorted. "Hardly."

"Well, I know it probably needs some flowers and stuff," Luke acknowledged, sipping the beer his future sister-in-law had offered him after the meal.

"We have to pick up chairs from the community center and set them up, then decorate the whole building with miles of pine garland and twinkling lights and big red bows."

"When you say *we*, you mean you and Annie, right?"

"Actually it was intended as a collective *we*," his

brother admitted. "As in, anyone I can convince to lend a hand."

"I can haul chairs," Luke decided. "But I'm not sure I'd have the first clue what to do with twinkling lights and bows."

"Me, neither," Danny admitted. Then, when Luke put his almost empty bottle on the table, he asked, "Do you want another beer?"

He shook his head. "I've had my limit."

"You've had one," his brother noted.

"That's my limit when I'm driving," he said.

Danny's brows lifted. "Since when?"

"Since the night that I got wasted and Mom and Dad were killed." He hadn't planned to blurt it out like that, but it was time—past time—for him to tell his brother the truth.

Danny rubbed his thumb through the condensation beaded on his can of soda. "Everything changed that night, didn't it?"

He nodded grimly. "And it was all my fault."

"What are you talking about?"

"The accident." Luke swallowed. "I think Mom and Dad were out that night because…because of me."

"Why would you think that?" his brother asked cautiously.

"Because it was late, and we were drunk. Well, I was drunk, and I'm pretty sure Bailey was, too. But not you. You weren't drinking."

"I was only eighteen," Danny reminded him.

"And always a rule follower. You wanted us to leave the bar," he suddenly remembered. "But we weren't ready to go. There were girls, and they were so friendly and pretty…and I was a drunken fool."

"It wasn't your fault," his brother said.

"Where the accident happened..." Even after a dozen years, remembering brought back all of the pain. Sure, he'd gone on with his life without his parents and without the rest of his family, but everything had changed that fateful night, and he knew that there would forever be an emptiness inside him because of it.

Danny waited for him to finish his thought, though he looked as uneasy as Luke felt about where this conversation was going.

"Where the accident happened," he began again. "I always figured they were so far away from home, so late at night, because they were looking for us." He scrubbed his hands over his face. "If I'd just listened to you, given you the keys and let you drive us home, that night might have ended differently. Everything might have ended differently."

His brother, eyes suspiciously bright, shook his head. "It wasn't your fault, Luke."

"How can you know that?"

"Because it was mine." Danny set his soda can down and stood up to pace restlessly across the room. "You're right about the fact that they were looking for us— because *I* called them. *I'm* the reason they were out on the road that night. It was my fault."

Luke was stunned by his brother's revelation—and not entirely sure he'd heard him correctly. "You called them?"

Danny nodded miserably.

He took a moment to absorb the implications of this admission, then realized it didn't change anything. He didn't believe for a minute that anything that happened was his brother's fault. Luke was the one who was responsible. He was the oldest and the undisputed leader whenever the three of them were out. If he'd made better choices, Danny would never have been put in the position of having to make such a call.

"But Annie's helped me to believe that maybe it wasn't my fault," Danny said when Luke remained silent. "That the fault lies with the driver of the vehicle that slammed into Dad's truck. Maybe my phone call was the reason they were on the road that night, but I'm not responsible for what happened to them."

"You're not," Luke agreed, eager to reassure his brother. "It wasn't your fault."

"And if it wasn't mine, then it wasn't yours, either," Danny said.

"Maybe," Luke allowed, desperate to trust that his brother was right but still unable—or unwilling—to let go of the guilt that he'd carried with him for so many years.

Because if he truly let himself believe that he wasn't responsible, then he'd simply be trading one set of regrets for another—namely that he'd stayed away from Rust Creek Falls and his family for all these years.

Chapter Eleven

Given a choice, Luke would choose to muck out stalls rather than battle crowds of holiday shoppers any day of the week. But since he'd decided to stay in Rust Creek Falls for Christmas—now less than a week away—he didn't really have that option.

Thankfully, he had Eva to keep him company and guide him through the labyrinth of stores. And though she'd insisted that they hit the road early in order to be at the mall in Kalispell when it opened on Wednesday, she had two large coffees and a bag of bear claws ready to go when he picked her up at the donut shop.

Fueled up on sugar and caffeine, they'd tackled his list with purpose and determination. A few hours later, when their arms were already weighed down with too many bags, he accepted yet another along with a cheery "Merry Christmas" from the sales clerk and fell into step behind Eva as they exited the store.

"That's it," she said as they carefully merged with the crowd of shoppers stampeding down the corridor.

"What's it?"

"You're finished," she told him. "Your list is done."

"I am? It is?"

She held up the list of names he'd written out and showed him the check marks she'd put beside each name as he'd purchased gifts.

"That's great," he said, and meant it. "Now we can tackle your list. You've done a lot of looking but you haven't bought anything."

"That's because I'm finished my Christmas shopping," she told him.

"You're finished already?"

"Christmas is in five days," she pointed out. "I would guess that most of the people here are finishing up, not just getting started."

"It's been a long time since I've had anyone to buy presents for—and celebrate the holidays with and I was feeling a little overwhelmed by the task."

"I think you came up with some really great ideas," she said encouragingly.

"Well, from what I've learned about the triplets, I suspect they'll be just as happy with the boxes as whatever is inside them."

"That's probably true," she acknowledged. "But I still think the toddler sports center was a good choice."

"And the box is big enough that Henry, Jared *and* Katie will all fit inside."

She laughed, easily picturing the scene he described. "It's a good thing you already took it out to your truck, or we wouldn't have been able to carry all of these other bags."

"Did I overdo it?" he asked.

"I don't think so. But now you have to wrap them."

"I never thought about that," he admitted.

"Which means that you need to get paper and tape and bows."

"Or I could take my gifts to that wrapping station at the center of the mall," he suggested as an alternative.

She shook her head. "That's not very personal—and it will cost you a fortune."

"But it will save me hours of wrangling with paper and tape and bows. Unless..." He deliberately left the rest of the thought unspoken.

"You're right—you don't know how to be subtle," Eva noted dryly. "But yes, I'll help with your wrapping."

Before Luke was willing to tackle that project, however, he told Eva that he needed food. So they picked up pizza and wings on their way back to his sister's house because as much as she appreciated his offer to buy dinner anywhere she wanted to go, what she really wanted was just to sit down and put her feet up for a while.

When the pizza box was empty and the wings were decimated to the bone, he cleared away the remnants of their dinner while Eva set up a wrapping station on Bella's enormous dining room table.

"I said I would help you with the wrapping—not that I would do it all," she pointed out to Luke a few hours later as he sat across from her, watching.

"Sorry," he said, not sounding sorry at all. "I'm too dazzled by your skill to concentrate on my task."

"Wrapping presents is hardly a skill. Besides, the only thing I asked you to do was measure and cut the paper."

"And I even screwed that up," he muttered.

She nodded and, unable to resist teasing him a little, remarked, "Impulsive penetration."

"Excuse me?"

"There's no need to apologize," she said soothingly. "It's a common rookie mistake."

His gaze narrowed. "Are we still talking about gift wrapping?"

She chuckled. "Yes, we're talking about gift wrapping—and the fact that you kept rushing to cut the paper without ensuring that it fit around the box."

"And that's…impulsive penetration?"

"Of course," she said with feigned innocence. "What did you think I was talking about?"

"I didn't want to imagine," he said dryly. "And now I've been demoted to bows."

"Bows *and* tags," she said, handing him the last box so that he could add those final touches. "Those tasks seem more in line with your experience."

"Where did you acquire your obviously vast experience?" he wondered aloud.

"Years of practice, including Presents for Patriots at the community center every Christmas."

"What's Presents for Patriots?" he asked.

"I keep forgetting that you've been gone for almost a dozen years," she admitted, loading up an armful of presents to add to the growing pile already under the Christmas tree in the family room. "It's a gift drive for our troops that started in Thunder Canyon and was adopted by Rust Creek Falls a few years back. Local individuals and businesses donate the presents and a few weeks before Christmas, volunteers gather at the community center to wrap them."

"And somehow, even with all the other demands on your time, you manage to participate in that, too."

"It's a good cause," she said.

"No doubt," he agreed, as he arranged the wrapped

packages beneath the tree. "But that doesn't add more hours to your day."

She shrugged. "Well, sleep is mostly overrated."

"You're an amazing woman, Eva Rose Armstrong."

"I'm not really."

He touched a finger to her lips, silencing her protest. "You are," he insisted. "Amazing...and irresistible."

Then his finger dropped away and his mouth covered hers.

His kiss was amazing and irresistible.

Not that Eva made any attempt to resist. Why would she when this was exactly what she wanted? *He* was exactly what she wanted.

And, finally, it seemed as if she was what he wanted, too.

Her lips parted willingly for him, and their tongues began to dance together in a sensual rhythm that made her heart pound and her knees tremble.

"Do you want to know the real reason that I offered to help wrap your presents?" she asked when he eased his lips from hers.

"Because you never say no when someone asks a favor?" he teased.

"Because I know you still have mixed feelings about being in Rust Creek Falls for Christmas and I wanted to help make some new and happy memories for you."

"Since we're sharing confessions, I have to admit that spending time with you has already made this holiday better than the last dozen."

The simple sincerity of his words filled her heart with joy and hope.

"Let's make it even better," she suggested, pulling his mouth down to hers again.

He didn't resist. The heat that had been simmering between them since the beginning had intensified over the past week. That heat spread through her veins now, so hot and fierce she melted against him.

As their tongues tangled together, his hands stroked leisurely up her back, then slowly down again. She shivered against him, an action that caused her already hardened nipples to brush the solid wall of his chest. A groan rumbled low in his throat as he clamped an arm behind her back and hauled her tight against him.

The unmistakable evidence of his arousal against her belly increased her own, and she rubbed wantonly against him. She had no interest in pretending that she didn't want to get naked with Luke. Right now she had no interest in anything but tearing his clothes off.

But when she reached for the top button of his shirt, he caught her wrists in his hands and held them. "As much as I want you, Eva, this isn't a good idea."

"Why not?"

"Because my time in Rust Creek Falls is limited," he reminded her gently.

"I know, and two weeks are already gone, so why are we wasting the time we have left?"

"You'd really be okay with a short-term relationship?"

"It wouldn't be my first choice," she admitted. "But if that's all you're willing to give me—"

"It's all I *can* give you."

"Then it's better than nothing."

He looked as if he was tempted to take what she was offering, but then he shook his head. "There's still so much you don't know about me, that if you did know, would make you understand why getting involved with me is a bad idea."

"So tell me."

* * *

For a lot of years, Luke had tried to not even think about what happened the night his parents were killed. He'd certainly never talked about it. That was, until a few days earlier when he'd finally confided in Danny— only to discover that his brother had never blamed Luke but had, instead, put the whole responsibility on his own shoulders.

It had been a little easier after that to tell it to Bella, who cried with her arms around him. Her tears were of grief, for everything they'd all lost, and somehow offered him a measure of healing he'd never expected. Then he'd told it again to Jamie, who'd reacted with considerably less affection but absolutely no judgment.

Now he needed to tell Eva. Before they took their relationship to the next level, she had a right to know the truth about who he was. She needed the whole truth in order to decide if she really wanted to be with him.

"It's not a story with a happy ending," he warned.

"Tell me anyway."

So he did.

He led her to the sofa and sat beside her, then told her the whole sordid story of what happened the night his parents were killed—how he'd been drinking at an out-of-town bar with his friends and his brothers, because Bailey would never be served in Rust Creek Falls where everyone knew that he wasn't yet twenty-one. He'd been having a great time, dancing with some of the pretty girls in the bar that night and simply loving life.

"How old were you?" Eva asked.

"Twenty-one," he admitted. "Bailey was twenty, Danny only eighteen."

"You've been beating yourself up for almost twelve

years over a mistake that you made when you were twenty-one?"

"That mistake changed everything."

"Maybe you exercised poor judgment that night," she acknowledged. "But you're not responsible for what happened to your parents."

He continued as if she hadn't spoken. "I was drunk, so a lot of my memories of that night are hazy—but only up until the part where a county sheriff came into the bar and told us about the accident." He dropped his head into his hands. "The funeral was—" he paused, searching for a word that could somehow sum up the gut-wrenching experience of standing shoulder to shoulder with his brothers and sisters to say a final goodbye to their parents. No word was adequate so he settled on "—awful."

Truthfully, he didn't remember much about the funeral, except that his tie had been knotted too tight at his throat, and his heart had felt like a lead weight in his chest. He didn't hear anything the minister said, because the words were drowned out by the echo of *my fault, my fault, my fault* over and over again inside Luke's head.

"After the funeral, we all went back to my grandparents' place. Matthew and Agnes Baldwin were my mom's parents—and they weren't happy about having the responsibility of even their youngest grandchildren thrust upon them, after making it clear that me and Bailey and Danny couldn't stay with them."

"That's when you left Rust Creek Falls," she realized.

He nodded. "We told ourselves that we were doing what was best for our younger siblings, believing that the grandparents would be able to handle four kids more easily than seven. But the truth was, I was grateful for the excuse to get away—from my own grief and guilt."

Eva touched a hand to his arm in a wordless gesture of support. He glanced at her, saw that her beautiful blue eyes shimmered with tears. But there was no judgment in her gaze, only sympathy and compassion—neither of which he deserved.

"We headed south and ended up in Wyoming, where we got hired on as ranch hands. We stuck together for a while…then we didn't.

"Danny and Bailey were all I had left of my family, but I let them go, too…because I felt like I deserved to lose everything and everyone who mattered to me."

Listening to the anguish in his tone, seeing the devastation in his eyes, nearly broke Eva's heart. But concerned that he might misinterpret her tears, she determinedly held them in check.

"It wasn't your fault, Luke," she told him, her tone sympathetic but firm. "And maybe that chapter of your life didn't have a happy ending, but it's not the end of your story. There are a lot more chapters still to be written. You get to decide on the ending you want."

"I've never had a serious relationship with a woman," he confided. "Anytime someone starts to get too close, I back away."

"You've lost a lot of people that you cared about," she acknowledged. "It's understandable that you'd be wary about falling in love."

"Maybe I'm not just wary. Maybe I'm not capable of loving anyone."

She didn't believe that. She wouldn't believe it. Luke had suffered more loss than any one person should ever have to, but she was confident that his return to Rust Creek Falls was the beginning of his healing. His family's support and understanding were only one key to the process. Another key was finding a woman that he could trust enough to open up his heart to love again, and she believed that she was that woman. Because she was already in love with him.

Of course, it was far too early to tell him that, so she decided to show him instead. She lifted her arms to his shoulders and rose on her toes to press her lips to his. "What time do you expect your sister and brother-in-law to be home?"

"They're gone until Friday," he admitted. "Hudson flew Bella to New York City to go ice-skating at Rockefeller Center."

"That's a long way to go to strap on a pair of skates."

"There was also something about shopping on Fifth Avenue and taking in a Broadway show. He's pulling out all the stops for their first Christmas as husband and wife."

"She's a lucky girl."

"Yes, she is," he agreed. "Now."

She lifted her hands to his face. He had that look in his eye, the one that told her he was still haunted by events from the past. She didn't want him thinking about the past. She wanted him in the here and now, with her.

She brushed her lips against his again. "What do you say we get lucky, too?"

Any lingering sadness in his eyes was pushed aside by heat. "I'm realizing now that I got luckier than I ever imagined the day I walked into Daisy's for a cup of coffee."

"Large. Black. To go." She recited the first words he'd said to her that day.

His lips curved, but the smile didn't quite edge the worry from his eyes. "Are you sure about this?"

She responded by lifting her sweater over her head and tossing it aside, then reached back to unzip her skirt so that it puddled at her feet, leaving her standing before him in only a white lace bra, bikini panties and stay-up stockings.

He swallowed. "I don't think we're going to make it upstairs to my bed," he warned. "Not this time."

She smiled, pleased by his response and satisfied that he was no longer fighting what they both wanted. "I don't want to go upstairs. I want you here. Now."

He yanked a blanket off the back of the sofa and spread it out on the floor. Then he reached for a remote on the mantel, pressed a couple of buttons and flames flickered to life in the hearth.

"Nice," she said approvingly.

"Very nice," he agreed, his eyes never leaving her body.

The heat in his gaze warmed her all over, but she stepped closer to the fire, closer to Luke. She splayed her hands on his chest and, even through the thick flannel of his shirt, she felt his heart beating, strong and steady, beneath her palms.

"You're a little overdressed," she told him.

This time, when she reached for his button, he made no move to stop her. Her fingers worked quickly, and she parted the fabric and pushed it over his shoulders, eager to put her hands on his bare skin—only to discover that he was wearing a long-sleeved thermal shirt beneath the flannel.

"It's winter in Montana," he explained, but he tugged the shirt over his head and tossed it aside. She hummed her approval as she slid her hands over his bare torso, her fingers tracing the ridges and ripples of his muscles, her nails scraping lightly over his skin.

He took her mouth in another hot, hungry kiss as she reached for the buckle of his belt, eager to help him discard the rest of his clothing. When he was completely and gloriously naked, he peeled the last scraps of lace from her body before easing her down onto the blanket and stretching out over her.

"You smell like a sugar cookie," he murmured as his lips moved over her jaw and down her throat, the stubble on his jaw scraping erotically against her skin. "And you taste even sweeter."

She didn't—couldn't—respond, because his hands were stroking boldly and confidently over her body, sending delicious shivers of sensation to her core and wiping all rational thought from her mind.

His calloused thumbs scraped over her rigid nipples, making her gasp with shocked pleasure. Then his mouth was at her breast, his tongue exploring the ultra-sensitive flesh. "Much, much sweeter."

His lips fastened around the tight peak. He suckled gently, and she moaned softly. Her fingers threaded through his hair, holding him in place against her breast, wordlessly encouraging him to continue. He suckled harder, and she moaned louder. Then he shifted his focus to her other breast and gave it the same close attention.

She couldn't remember when she'd last been with a man, except that it had been a very long time. So long that she'd almost forgotten how good a man's hands could feel on her body. But Luke was reminding her now. So long that she'd almost forgotten how good a man's body could feel under her hands. But she was remembering now. While he continued to taste and tease her breasts, she reached a hand between their bodies and wrapped her fingers around his hard, velvety length. This time, he moaned.

She rocked her hips against his, wordlessly telling him what she wanted, what she needed. He rummaged around on the floor until he found his discarded jeans and pulled a condom out of his wallet.

"You must have been a boy scout," she said, partly teasing but mostly grateful that he was prepared for what was about to happen.

"I can tie you up in forty different ways, if that's your thing," he told her.

She laughed as she took the square packet from his hand and carefully tore it open. "Forty ways, huh?"

"Well, I used to know forty ways," he amended. "Now I probably only remember about half of them."

"Let's save that for another time, then," she suggested, carefully unrolling the prophylactic over his erection. "Right now, I don't want props or tricks. I only want you."

"And I want you," he said, rising over her and, finally, easing into her.

"Oh." She closed her eyes on a sigh of pure pleasure as he stretched and filled her, a glorious tension beginning to build deep inside her.

His lips brushed against hers. "Okay?"

She opened her eyes to find his on her.

"Okay," she confirmed.

He kissed her again, his tongue mirroring the intimate strokes of his body as he began to move.

Her hands glided over him, her fingers tracing the contours of his muscles, digging into his shoulders as, with each thrust, he pushed her closer and closer to the edge.

She held on to him, her anchor in the storm of sensations that battered at her from all directions.

She couldn't think; she couldn't speak; she could only feel. And the way he was moving inside her felt so good she never wanted him to stop. The pleasure continued to build with each stroke until it was an almost unbearable pressure inside her, almost more than she could stand.

Then…finally…release.

As her body shuddered with the aftershocks of pleasure, he groaned deeply and let his own climax take him.

Chapter Twelve

"Best. Christmas. Present. Ever."

Several minutes later, when Luke's brain was capable of functioning again, they were the first words that came to mind. They spilled out of his mouth uncensored, surprising a laugh out of Eva.

She lifted herself up on an elbow and smiled at him. "It was pretty spectacular, wasn't it?"

He stroked a hand leisurely down her torso, loving the softness of her skin—and the nakedness of her body. "I'm not ever going to be able to look at this tree without thinking about you and what we did here tonight."

"Good."

"And when my sister asks, on Christmas morning, why I've got a goofy smile on my face, I'll tell her to ask you."

She was still smiling, too, as she shifted away from him and began to gather up her clothes.

He found her panties before she did and held on when she tried to tug them from his grasp.

"I'm going to need those," she told him.

"Not just yet."

She lifted a brow. "When?"

"Later." He pulled her close and kissed her. "Much later."

But instead of easing her back onto the blanket, he lifted her into his arms.

"Where are you taking me?" she demanded.

"Upstairs."

"Why?"

"Because I want to make love to you in a bed...very slowly...and very thoroughly...and without worrying about bruises on your back or friction burns on my knees."

"That sounds like an incredibly appealing idea," she agreed as he effortlessly carried her up the stairs.

"I was hoping you'd think so." He tumbled with her onto the bed, straddling her hips with his knees and catching her lips in another mind-numbing kiss.

"You're really good at that," she said when he eased his lips away. "Which makes me wonder..."

He nuzzled the sweet spot below her ear. "What are you wondering?"

"How it is that..." She momentarily lost her train of thought when he nipped at her earlobe, then nibbled his way down the side of her throat, raising goose bumps on her skin and sending shivers of excitement coursing through her veins.

"You were saying?" he prompted.

"How is it that you can tie twenty different knots in a piece of rope—" she sucked in a breath when his hand slid down to the apex of her thighs and embarked on a leisurely exploration, but she made a valiant effort to finish her thought "—but you can't wrap paper around a box?"

"Is that really what's on your mind right now?" he

asked, his tone colored with amusement as he continued his sensual exploration.

"Right now my mind is pretty much blank," she admitted. "But earlier… I was trying to make sense of the… dichotomy."

"We all have different talents," he told her.

"Apparently," she said as he zeroed in on the bull's-eye and, within minutes, sent her soaring.

"That was a pretty impressive display of talent," she commented when she'd finally managed to catch her breath and form a coherent thought again.

"That was just the warm-up," he said.

And he proceeded to prove it to her.

"What time is it?"

Luke opened one eye to glance at the glowing numbers of the clock on the bedside table. "Almost midnight," he said in answer to Eva's sleepy question.

"It feels so much later."

"We've had a busy day." And hers had been even busier, as she'd started the morning baking at Daisy's.

"But a good day," she said, a smile in her voice.

"A very good day," he confirmed.

After another few minutes, just as he was starting to think that she might have fallen asleep, she spoke again. "I should go."

"I wish you didn't have to," he said, surprised to realize it was true. While he wasn't ready to analyze his feelings too deeply, there was something about being with Eva that just felt…right.

And though their lovemaking had been beyond spectacular, he didn't just mean between the sheets. He truly enjoyed spending time with her—wherever they were and whatever they were doing.

He'd never enjoyed shopping. And, for the past dozen years, he hadn't enjoyed Christmas, either. The season that brought families together only served to remind him that his family had been torn apart—that he'd torn his family apart.

Now, with Eva, he actually felt as if he might be able to move past his grief and his guilt.

But even if he finally managed to dump the emotional baggage that had weighed him down for so long, he suspected that his heart would still bear the effects, like the bowed back of a pack horse never relieved of his burden. But when he was with Eva, he almost believed that she could fix whatever was broken inside him. In fact, he almost believed that, if she could love him, maybe he was worthy of being loved.

"I wish I didn't have to go, either," she said. "But I need at least a few hours' sleep before I have to be at work."

He wanted to suggest that she could sleep right where she was, but he knew that she couldn't. While her mom and dad seemed to respect that she was a grown woman, he was sure they wouldn't approve of her spending the whole night in a man's bed. And although he would prefer to stay exactly where he was, with Eva's naked body in his arms, he didn't want to cause any conflict in her relationship with her parents.

"And people think that ranchers work crazy hours," he noted.

"I don't mind the early mornings," she said. "In fact, I like being in the kitchen when it's quiet, watching the sun rise as I sip my first cup of coffee."

"I'd need *gallons* of coffee."

She smiled at that. "I'm well aware of your caffeine addiction."

"And even with gallons of coffee, I'm not sure I'd make it through the day," he admitted.

"I sometimes sneak a nap in the afternoon," she confided.

"Why don't you sneak over here so that we can have that *nap* together?"

She laughed. "When I say *nap*, it's not some kind of code. I actually mean *sleep*. Besides, aren't you supposed to be helping at Sunshine Farm tomorrow?"

"I'd much rather nap with you," he told her.

"I appreciate the thought," she said. "But right now, I'd really appreciate a ride home."

It was 12:39 a.m. when he pulled into the driveway of her house, and she exhaled a grateful sigh of relief when she saw that the porch light was on but the living room was dark—confirmation that her parents had already turned in for the night. Though her parents weren't thrilled about the amount of time she was spending with Luke, she knew that they wouldn't express any outward disapproval. But she also suspected that her mother would take one look at her and know she'd had sex, and Eva wanted to keep that joyous event to herself for just a little while longer.

So she unlocked the door, turned to wave goodbye to Luke, then tiptoed up the stairs to her bedroom.

When he got back to his sister's house, he sent her a text message to let her know, and she hugged the phone to her chest where her heart was beating in a crazy erratic rhythm, like some kind of cardiac Morse code that spelled out her feelings for him.

He'd been completely honest and up-front with her about his plans—and he didn't plan to stay in Rust Creek Falls. She'd known that before she kissed him the first time, but what she knew in her head didn't hold much sway over her heart. She'd fallen in love with him anyway. All the way, head over heels in love.

But even if she ended up with her heart broken, she wouldn't regret giving it to him. She still hoped that he might change his mind about leaving and decide to make Rust Creek Falls his home once again, but if he didn't, she hoped he would look back on the time he'd spent with her and smile at the memories they'd made together.

The bed that Luke had been sleeping in, comfortably and soundly, for the past two weeks, suddenly seemed cold and empty without Eva beside him. He wished she could have stayed the night—so that he could make love to her one more time before they fell asleep and again in the morning.

But he understood why she had to leave. Not just because she lived with her parents but because she was a part of the community. He couldn't blame her for not wanting everyone to know that she'd gotten naked with "the oldest Stockton boy"—as he was referred to by many residents.

Maybe it would be different if he planned to stay in Rust Creek Falls, but he didn't and it wasn't. So he would take whatever moments she would give him, enjoy whatever pleasures they found together. At some point last night, he'd decided to accede to his sister's request—and his own desire—to stay through the holidays. But after the New Year, he would go back to Cheyenne as he'd originally planned.

He fell asleep, refusing to admit—even to himself—that there was a part of him that wanted to change that plan.

And he dreamed of Eva.

Eva was seriously tempted to hit the snooze button when her alarm beeped only a few hours later. Unfortunately, the donuts and pastries wouldn't bake themselves, so she forced her weary body out of bed and stumbled to the shower. She closed her eyes as the hot water poured over her, easing the unfamiliar stiffness in her muscles.

Not that she was complaining. Not at all. Because aside from a few aches, she felt good. Better than good. For the first time in a long time, her body felt sated.

It was her heart that continued to yearn.

She'd promised Luke that she didn't want anything more than he was offering, because she'd wanted it to be true. But she'd lied, perhaps to herself as much as to him, though that had never been her intention. She hadn't known, maybe hadn't wanted to know, that her heart had already opened to him, wholly and completely.

Unfortunately, his heart was still intent on heading back to Wyoming after the holidays—and the New Year was now less than two weeks away. Which meant that she needed to make Luke fall in love with her before those two weeks were up. A daunting task, perhaps.

Or maybe—her lips curved as a plan began to take shape in her mind—a piece of cake.

Eva decided that cookies were more practical than cake, and she was carrying a tin when she walked into the barn where Danny and Annie were planning to get married. There had been a lot of volunteers at the property over the past few days as they raced against the clock to get the venue ready for the big event. Today, however, there were only a few vehicles parked by the barn, which suggested that either the work was almost done or the crew had given up.

When she muscled open the door and stepped inside the cavernous space, she knew that her first guess had been correct.

"Wow," Eva said. "This place looks great."

Luke stepped down off the ladder he'd been perched on and crossed the room to meet her. "*You* look great," he said. "This place looks like a barn."

"Because it is a barn," she reminded him.

"Uh-huh." He dipped his head and touched his lips to hers. "I thought you were going to nap this afternoon."

"I was, and then I thought that the bride and groom might need a couple of extra hands—"

"Always," Annie interjected.

"—and a snack to keep everyone going."

"Snack?" Danny echoed hopefully.

Eva pried the lid off the tin.

"You mentioned sugar cookies yesterday," she reminded Luke, and though her words were deliberately vague, the mischievous twinkle in her eye told him that she had a clear and specific memory about when and where he'd been thinking about the treats. "So when I was baking this morning, I made an extra batch to bring out here."

"That was incredibly thoughtful," Annie said, peering into the tin at the snowflake-shaped cookies decorated with glossy icing and colored sugars. "Oh, but they almost look too pretty to eat."

"No, they don't," her fiancé denied, reaching over her shoulder to pluck one from the tin. "But they taste as good as they look," he said around a mouthful of cookie.

Annie rolled her eyes, but she chose one and nibbled on a corner. "Oh, these are good," she said. "Maybe we should have opted for cookies rather than cake for the wedding."

"Cake is traditional," Danny noted as he reached for another cookie.

"It's about the only part of our wedding that is," Annie pointed out. "Well, that and the bride in a white dress."

"Speaking of which," her fiancé said, pulling his cell phone out of his pocket to check the time, "we're supposed to pick up your dress at the bridal shop in Kalispell this afternoon."

Annie cast a critical glance around the room. "Or *I* could go there while *you* string up the lights here."

"I could help Luke with the lights," Eva volunteered.

"It's a big job," Annie said worriedly.

"I think we can figure it out," Luke told her. "If not, I'm sure there are sketches in your wedding folder."

The bride-to-be's cheeks flushed, confirming the accuracy of his guess.

"Are you sure you don't mind?" Annie asked.

"They're sure," Danny said, taking her arm to steer her toward the door, eager to make his escape.

But he did pause long enough to grab a few more cookies from the tin on his way out.

"Wedding folder?" Eva asked when they'd gone.

Luke shook his head. "You don't want to know."

She helped herself to a cookie. "I thought there would

be more people here. I didn't realize the work was almost done."

"I guess that means more cookies for us."

She put the lid back on the tin. "*After* the lights are done."

"While I appreciate the offer of help, it's not really a difficult job so if you don't want to stay—"

"I do want to stay," she said.

A few hours later, the muscles in her shoulders and arms were protesting her decision as she reached up to catch the final coil of lights that Luke dropped from the top of the ladder. "It's been fun to watch this place transform from a livestock shelter to a wedding venue."

"All the twinkling lights in the world aren't going to make this place look like anything but a barn with twinkling lights," he said as he began his descent. "And why anyone would want to get married in a barn is beyond me."

"Maybe the location has some special significance to them," she suggested. "Perhaps the first time he kissed her was in this barn. Or maybe the first time they made love was in the hay loft."

Luke held up his hands. "Enough speculation. I don't really want to know."

She laughed as she looped the lights over a nail that had been hammered into the wall for that purpose. But the laugh cut off as she sucked in a breath.

He was immediately at her side. "What happened?"

"Splinter," she said.

He took her hand and gently unfolded the fingers that had instinctively curled into a fist. "That's a big one. And it seems to be in pretty deep."

"Are you talking about my hand or trying to evoke memories of last night?"

"It's not a good idea to distract me with dirty talk when you're wounded," he chastised.

"It's just a little wood."

His gaze narrowed. "Definitely *not* what you were saying last night."

She laughed. "Can you get it out? Please."

"Again, not words I've heard you say before." But his expression grew serious as he turned his attention back to her hand. "You should have been wearing gloves."

"I'm not a delicate flower," she told him.

He stroked his thumb along the side of her palm, sending tingles shooting up her arm and down her spine. "Your hands are soft."

Because she pampered them before bed every night, using a special scrub and lotion to ensure they didn't bear evidence of the arduous work they did in the kitchen. "And strong."

He nodded, acknowledging the fact. "I've seen you lift fifty-pound bags of flour as effortlessly as an angel food cake," he agreed. "But you should still be careful."

"It's a splinter," she reminded him. "Not a bullet wound."

Though it wasn't lodged completely under her skin, his fingers were too big and clumsy to be able to grasp the end and pull it free.

"There used to be a first-aid kit in the tack room," Luke remembered. "I might find a pair of tweezers in there."

"Let's take a look."

He continued to hold her hand as he led her toward the back of the barn.

She hadn't been in the tack room before, but someone had obviously done a thorough job sweeping the space free of dust and cobwebs. Eva might have grown up in town, but she was enough of a country girl to recognize the faint scents of saddle soap, beeswax and leather—with just a hint of wood smoke, courtesy of the old stove in the corner—that lingered in the air.

Beneath a row of bridle hooks, empty saddle racks hung on the wall. On another wall, there were benches and shelves. A row of wooden boxes was lined up on the lowest shelf, and Luke instinctively reached for the nearest one and pulled it down.

"Here we go," he said, lifting out a smaller white box with a familiar red cross on the cover.

"That doesn't look as if it's been in here for at least a dozen years," Eva noted with relief.

"Whoever cleaned up in here must have replaced the old one," Luke said.

"Probably Annie," she surmised. "Moms appreciate the importance of having antibacterial cream and Band-Aids on hand."

"Hopefully tweezers, too," he said, unsnapping the lid. He rifled through the contents. "Even better—individually wrapped sterile splinter removers."

He opened the package and lifted out the instrument, then reached for her hand again. She was aware of his palm—wide and calloused—beneath her hand, and she found herself remembering how those strong, hard hands felt sliding over her naked skin, skimming over her curves, caressing her—

"Did I hurt you?"

She blinked. "What?"

"You shivered," he said. "And I thought maybe I hurt you."

"No," she said, her cheeks flushing beneath his scrutiny. "I guess I just…um…got a chill."

"Well, it's out."

"Out?" she echoed, uncomprehending.

His lips twitched at the corners. "The splinter."

She looked down at her hand, still cradled gently in his, and saw that the sliver of wood had, indeed, been removed from her palm, leaving only a small red mark where it had been. She started to draw her hand away, but he held it still.

"You still need some antibiotic cream and a Band-Aid."

"It was just a splinter."

"It was a big splinter and it was wedged deep."

And yet, she hadn't even felt him pull it out of her skin, because her mind had been too busy spinning romantic fantasies.

Still holding her hand, he lowered his head and pressed his lips to her palm. Her breath hitched.

"A kiss to make it better," he said.

"Should I give you a list of all the other places that hurt?"

He smiled and released her hand to unwrap a Band-Aid and dab some cream on the pad, then carefully place it over her wound. "The first time I ever kissed a girl was in this room," he told her as he worked.

"Was it?"

"Charmaine Wilson. I was twelve, she was fourteen."

"An older woman," she mused aloud.

He nodded. "She wore her long, dark hair in a single braid down her back, skin-tight jeans and she had the most amazing br—" he cleared his throat "—brown eyes."

Eva chuckled. "And how long did your infatuation with Charmaine Wilson last?"

"Almost a whole week."

"You did tell me that long-term relationships aren't your thing," she acknowledged.

"So why are you still hanging around with me?"

"I happen to enjoy your company." She dropped her voice to a conspiratorial whisper. "And the off-the-charts sex."

"I think we're done here for today," he decided as he drew her into his embrace. "It's Thursday, isn't it?"

"All day," she confirmed.

"Does that mean your parents are bowling tonight?"

"It does," she said, impressed that he'd remembered.

"So what would you say if I suggested that we grab a bite before going back to my sister's place?"

"I'd say 'yes, please.'"

Over the past twelve years, Luke had almost forgotten what it meant to be part of a family. In only a few weeks, being around Bella and Hudson, Danny and Annie and Janie, and Jamie and Fallon and HJK—as his youngest brother fondly and collectively referred to his triplets— had reminded him and shown him how much better life was with people he cared about and who cared about him. Which made him think that maybe he should forget his promise to stay in Rust Creek Falls until after Danny's wedding, until after the New Year, and head back to Wyoming now, before he started to feel as if he belonged here.

That would be the smart thing to do, but it wasn't what he wanted to do.

In fact, the prospect of going back to Wyoming was surprisingly unappealing. He didn't want to walk away from the siblings he'd just started to reconnect with, and he didn't want to leave the woman who had already taken hold of his heart.

Chapter Thirteen

Eva couldn't remember a time in her life when she'd been happier than she was with Luke. Her euphoric mood was dimmed only by the fact that Luke hadn't said anything to her about his plans for the New Year. Or rather that he hadn't said anything that suggested he'd change his plans.

Because the truth was that he'd clearly—and repeatedly—told her of his intention to return to Cheyenne after the holidays, but Eva kept waiting for him to realize that he wanted a future with her and decide to stay in Rust Creek Falls so that they could build a life together. So far, he'd remained silent on the topic, so she'd pushed the questions and concerns aside and focused on preparing for the holidays—and spending every possible minute with the man she loved.

"Your dad and I are going to watch *White Christmas* tonight," Marion told Eva after dinner on Friday. "Do you and Luke want to join us?"

She appreciated that her mom had included Luke in the invitation, but she shook her head. "We're going to the Ace in the Hole. Rosey's hosting another viewing party to show the final episode of *The Great Roundup*. Practically the whole town is going to be there."

"That will be quite the crowd," Marion said. "Why don't you watch it here?"

"Aside from the fact that you want to watch *White Christmas*, Dad can't watch anything without the clicker in his hand, changing channels every few minutes to ensure he isn't missing something better on another station."

Her mother sighed, unable to deny the fact. "We're supposed to get another storm tonight. Please keep an eye on the weather and come home early if it gets bad."

"I'll keep an eye on the weather," she promised.

But the concerned expression remained on her mother's face as she continued to dry and put the dishes away.

"What are you really worried about, Mom?"

Marion folded the towel and hung it over the handle of the oven door. "That you'll marry Luke and move to Wyoming," she finally said.

Eva was stunned. "Why would you ever think something like that?"

"Because I know you're in love with him, and I'm beginning to suspect, considering the amount of time he's been spending with you, that he has some pretty deep feelings, too."

She hoped her mother was right about Luke's feelings, but right now she was more concerned about Marion's. "Where's this coming from, Mom?"

"I guess I was just thinking about how much has changed over the past few years—and how much more is going to change."

"What do you mean? Is Dad—"

"Your father's fine," Marion hastened to assure her.

"He's really, truly fine. I'm sorry—you know I always get emotional around the holidays."

Eva smiled. "I know. You don't only cry during holiday movies, you cry over the commercials."

"Some of them," her mother acknowledged. "But as I was digging through the holiday movies, looking for *White Christmas*, I was thinking about all the times we watched it together as a family. Then Calla got married and moved away, and Delphine got married and moved away, and…well, you're the only one I have left."

"I'm not going anywhere," Eva assured her.

But Marion shook her head. "I don't want you to make those kinds of promises. Don't get me wrong—I would miss you terribly if you went away, but you have to live your own life. Follow your heart."

"I will, but I'll always be here if you need me."

"I know." Her mother hugged her tight. "But right now, you need to get ready for your date."

"I still can't believe that Brenna and Travis are actually married," Eva remarked to Luke as they left the Ace later that night.

"That certainly seemed to be a big surprise ending to the season," he agreed.

She knew he hadn't really followed the series, insisting that the only reality TV he was interested in was live-action football. She also knew that, as a result of being in Rust Creek Falls over the past few weeks, he'd been caught up in the fervor.

"I'll bet it was a surprise to both their families, too. Although Travis is several years older than Brenna, they've known each other forever, and I don't think anyone ever suspected there were sparks between them."

"Sometimes there needs to be friction to generate sparks," Luke commented, opening the passenger door of his truck for her.

"I guess that's true," she acknowledged, still stunned by the revelation of the on-set wedding. But maybe she shouldn't have been surprised to learn that the gorgeous hairdresser and sexy cowboy had found love on the reality show. Over the past few months a lot of romances had blossomed in Rust Creek Falls.

Eva loved a happy ending as much as anyone, and while she was sincerely pleased for the newlyweds, she couldn't help but feel a little envious, too. She was grateful that she'd met Luke, and getting to know him had inevitably led to falling in love with him, but she was still waiting for some hint or indication that he felt the same way. Because as exciting as it was to be in love, she wanted to be loved, too.

Luke turned onto Cedar Street, then reached across the center console to take her hand. "Is everything okay?"

"Of course," she replied automatically.

"Are you sure? Because you've been quiet since we left the Ace."

"I'm just tired," she said.

And she was—physically and emotionally. The early mornings at Daisy's took a toll on her body, but it was her heart and spirit that were really feeling beaten down. Tired of being left out. Tired of helping other people plan their weddings—which reminded her, "And I still have to finish making the flowers for Danny and Annie's wedding cake."

"Speaking of their wedding," Luke said. "Annie's been stressing about making sure there are enough seats at the wedding and she wants to know if I'm going to have a 'plus one.'"

"Are you asking me to be your 'plus one'?"

"I know it's Christmas Eve and your sisters will be here with their families so you're probably busy…"

"Just ask the question, Luke," she interjected.

He smiled at the impatience in her tone, "Will you go to Danny and Annie's Christmas Eve wedding with me? I can't recommend the venue, but the cake should be good."

"I would love to," she said.

"This must be a director's cut," Eva commented when she walked into the house and found her parents snuggled together on the sofa watching the end of *White Christmas*.

"One of the benefits of watching a movie on Blu-ray is being able to pause it to make popcorn or take bathroom breaks," her dad commented, hitting the pause button again.

"Or to watch the final episode of *The Great Roundup* and the postshow reunion," Marion added.

Eva smiled. "I wondered if you would switch over."

"I wanted to find out if Brenna and Travis were still together," her mom admitted. "And your dad wanted to know who took the prize money."

"And now you know that Brenna was the big winner," Eva noted. "She got the money and her man."

"I'll bet there was a lot of buzz at the Ace when Travis and Brenna admitted they were married for real."

"There was, but that wasn't the only buzz," Eva said, then proceeded to tell them that Phil Dalton had bought a huge parcel of land on the outskirts of town.

"I knew he'd been looking for some property around here," Ray admitted.

"After losing his home and his wife in January, it's understandable that he'd want a fresh start," Marion noted.

"His sons, too," she said. "Apparently they're going to live on and work the land with him."

"That's wonderful news," her mother said. "During times of tragedy, it's more important than ever for families to stick together."

Eva agreed, and she knew that Luke was still feeling the effects of losing touch with his siblings after the deaths of their parents.

"There are rumors going around that some of Neal Dalton's kids are planning to move to Rust Creek Falls, too," she said.

"Phil could use the extra hands," Ray commented.

"And the support of more family close by," Marion added.

And because spending time with Luke had helped Eva recognize and appreciate the value of her family, she settled onto the sofa and watched the end of *White Christmas* with her parents.

All of the guests agreed that the newly refurbished barn at Sunshine Farm was a beautiful setting for a Christmas Eve wedding. Only those who had been involved with the intense rehab efforts over the past few weeks could truly appreciate the transformation that had been effected. Eva had pitched in a little herself, but even she was awed by the end result.

His two sisters that the groom had reconnected with stood up with the bride. Though Dana hadn't lived in Rust Creek Falls since she was a child, Annie knew how much his siblings meant to her soon-to-be husband, so she'd chosen to involve them in the ceremony as much as possible. Bella and Dana were dressed in long-sleeve, scoop-neck gowns of dark green velvet. The flower girl—Danny and Annie's daughter, Janie—was wearing a matching style in red. All three of the attendants carried bouquets of red roses with festive accents of evergreen, pinecones and berries.

The bride's dress was silk taffeta with a lace overlay. Annie had confided to Eva—who wanted to match the icing on the cake to the color of the bride's dress—that she had reservations about wearing white, and although her dress was technically ivory, she worried that tongues would wag. But when she took her first steps down the makeshift aisle, Eva didn't imagine anyone was thinking anything except that she was a truly beautiful bride.

The ceremony was an interesting mix of traditional and nontraditional elements. Instead of walking down the aisle on the arm of her father, the bride was given away by her ex-husband. Unorthodox, perhaps, but considering that Annie and Hank were both committed to continuing to co-parent the daughter they'd raised together from birth, it was a gesture that spoke to the bond of their family.

Dana had arrived in Rust Creek Falls the night before, taking up Bella's offer of a spare bedroom, and Luke had stayed up late with her, as if a few extra hours might somehow allow him to catch up on everything he'd missed over the past twelve years. At first it had been difficult to reconcile the little girl he remembered with the young woman who walked into Bella's living room. Then Dana smiled at him, and it was the smile he remembered. The sparkle in her eyes was the sparkle he remembered. And it felt so good to see her again, even if it hurt to think about all the years he'd lost, all the moments they'd never shared.

Now, as he stood between the groom and his youngest brother and watched the bride make her way down the aisle, he felt an array of emotions. Happiness for his brother, who was finally marrying the woman he'd always loved. Gratitude that Hudson's PI had found him and convinced him to make the long journey to Rust Creek Falls. And pride that the prettiest woman at the wedding—aside from the bride, of course—was his date.

The only disappointment was that the entire family wasn't there to witness the nuptials. He had long ago accepted that his parents were gone forever, but he keenly felt the absence of Bailey and Liza, and he was sure it was the same for each of his brothers and sisters in attendance. But no one was letting their absence put a damper on the occasion, and the smile on Danny's face as he watched his bride make her way toward him could have lit the whole barn without the hundreds of twinkling lights.

When the minister asked the assembled guests if there was any reason the bride and groom should not be joined together, a deep voice called out from the back. "Well, it just doesn't seem right for Danny to get married without all of his brothers as witnesses to the big event."

The bride sent a panicked glance toward her groom, obviously shocked that anyone would speak up in response to the question. Almost as quickly, the meaning of the words became clear, and her shocked surprise turned to pleasure.

It took Danny another half a second to put the pieces together after he turned from his bride to face the back of the barn. "Bailey?"

The latecomer took a few steps closer to the happy couple. "I think my invitation must have gotten lost in the mail."

"It must have," Danny agreed. Then he gave his bride's hands a light squeeze before releasing them and turning to embrace his brother. "Glad you could make it."

"Me, too."

Jamie was next in line to hug his long-lost brother, apparently not harboring any lingering animosity toward this particular sibling. "When did you get into town?"

"Just about half an hour ago," Bailey told him, turning to embrace Bella.

"Where are you staying?" she asked, wiping tears from her eyes. "Because we've got plenty of room at our place."

"I can attest to that," Dana said, edging forward to hug him next.

"But we can probably work out those details *after* the ceremony," Luke suggested. "Because there's a pretty girl in a white dress waiting patiently for the groom to put a ring on her finger."

"Not quite so patiently," Annie admitted.

"I've waited a lot of years to see you again," Danny said to Bailey. "But I've waited even longer to make Annie my wife, so it would be great if we could move forward with the ceremony now."

The guests laughed as the groom resumed his place beside the bride.

"Does anyone have anything else to say?" the minister asked the assembled guests.

This time there was no response, and the officiant resumed his duties.

And despite the whispers and speculation sparked by

Bailey's unexpected arrival, the focus of attention returned to the happy couple.

Eva watched through eyes blurred with tears as the bride and groom exchanged vows, promising to love, honor and cherish one another "till death do us part." The words were no different than those spoken by countless couples at countless weddings, but having at least a little bit of knowledge of what Annie and Danny had been through, the events that had torn them apart and, finally, brought them together again, made the promises that much more poignant.

It was an emotional day for all of the Stockton siblings—or at least all of those who were present. Having Bailey show up in time to witness the exchange of vows was undoubtedly sweeter than the icing on the wedding cake, but Eva suspected they were all aware of the absence of Liza, the little sister who had yet to be found.

After the ceremony, there was much eating and drinking and toasting the happy couple. Then the bride and groom cut the cake before taking to the makeshift dance floor for their first dance. As Eva listened to Dierks Bentley claim "there ain't nothing that love can't fix," she crossed her fingers that it was true. For Annie and Danny, of course, but also for her and Luke.

She knew that love couldn't magically obliterate the geographical distance between Cheyenne and Rust Creek Falls, but she had to hope and believe that Luke would acknowledge his feelings for her and reconsider his decision to leave after the New Year.

"What thoughts have you looking as if you're a hundred miles away?" Luke wondered.

She felt her cheeks flush, embarrassed to have been

caught daydreaming and unwilling to admit to Luke that he was the subject of those daydreams. "I was just thinking about Danny and Annie," she said. "They really are living proof that love can last."

His gaze shifted to the couple on the dance floor. "He never wanted to leave Rust Creek Falls—or Annie."

She reached up and touched a hand to his face, drawing his attention back to her. "That's not on you, Luke."

"Isn't it?" he asked, his tone heavy with regret.

"He made his own decision," she insisted.

"He was an eighteen-year-old kid who'd just lost his parents," Luke reminded her. "So he followed the lead of his oldest brother and left the only woman he'd ever loved."

"He was only eighteen—how could you possibly know that she was the only woman he'd ever love?" she challenged.

"Maybe I couldn't," he allowed.

"And you certainly couldn't have known that Annie was pregnant," she said, anticipating his next argument. "Not even Annie knew she was pregnant when you and Bailey and Danny left Rust Creek Falls."

"That's true," he acknowledged.

"So why don't you forget about the past and focus on the present—like they're doing," she suggested.

"I never used to believe in the mystical power of love," he told her. "Then I came back to Rust Creek Falls and I saw Bella with Hudson, Jamie with Fallon, and Danny with Annie." As he spoke, his gaze searched the room, finding each of his siblings and their partners in turn, before returning to meet Eva's eyes again. "And I met you."

With those words, she felt as if her heart actually

swelled inside her chest. "My life changed when you came back to Rust Creek Falls, too," she admitted.

"In a good way, I hope."

"In all the very best ways," she assured him.

Luke smiled. "I'm glad, because I've been thinking that—"

Chapter Fourteen

Before Luke could finish his thought, Bailey brought a hand down on his brother's shoulder, effectively cutting off the words Eva desperately wanted to hear.

"I had no idea, when I decided to make the trip to Rust Creek Falls, that I'd show up just in time for Danny's wedding," Bailey said.

She managed to keep the smile on her face, though what she really wanted to do was lift both her hands to Bailey's chest and shove him aside so that she and Luke could finish their private conversation.

"The best wedding present you could have given him," Luke told his brother.

Bailey glanced at Eva. "Was I interrupting something?"

Yes, she wanted to shout at him.

But she knew that Luke was thrilled to see his brother again, so she pushed aside her own disappointment and said, "Nothing that can't wait."

She hoped.

"In fact, I was just going to excuse myself to get a glass of punch."

"Let me get it for you," Luke suggested.

But she shook her head. "You stay and chat with your brother. I'm sure you have lots to catch up on."

"We do," Bailey responded before Luke could. "Thanks for understanding."

She nodded and slipped away.

Luke watched Eva go, admiring the mouthwatering display of shapely leg as she moved through the crowd toward the makeshift bar. In the few weeks that he'd known her, he'd rarely seen her in anything other than the long, flowing skirts she obviously favored. Today she was wearing a blue dress that deepened the color of her eyes and hugged her every curve, with shiny black platform heels that added several inches to her height.

He watched as she helped herself to a glass of punch, then turned to smile at something Hank said to her. He didn't blame the man for the way his gaze followed Eva as she turned away, but he didn't like it, either.

"Looks like I got here just in time," Bailey noted.

Luke forced his attention back to his brother. "It meant a lot to Danny that you were able to be here for his wedding."

"He seems happy enough—for now," Bailey said.

"What's that supposed to mean?"

"Just that the rose-colored glasses tend to get wiped clean after the honeymoon."

"I did notice that your wife doesn't seem to have made the trip with you," Luke commented.

"*Ex*-wife," Bailey said grimly.

He winced. "I'm sorry."

His brother shrugged. "It turned out that marriage wasn't quite what I expected."

"What did you expect?"

Bailey lifted his beer to his lips, took a long sip. "Till death do us part."

"What changed?"

"I couldn't be the kind of husband Emily wanted me to be—that I wanted to be." He swallowed another mouthful of beer. "Hell, Luke, you know as well as I do that the scars of the past never go away. Even when, on the surface, it looks like they've healed, the wounds still ache deep inside."

Luke frowned, not wanting to believe what his brother said, though the words closely echoed his own thoughts. "Danny seems to be doing okay," he noted.

"Maybe because he loved Annie before everything went to hell in a handbasket," Bailey suggested.

"What even is a handbasket?" Luke wondered aloud.

His brother chuckled, though the sound was without humor. "I have no clue."

"You really don't think they'll make it?"

Bailey looked out at the dance floor where the newly-weds swayed together to the music, oblivious to everyone and everything around them. "I hope they do, but I don't think the odds are in their favor."

"Don't tell that to the groom."

"I wouldn't," his brother promised. "But I felt it was important to tell you."

"Why?"

"Because I saw the way you were looking at the pretty blonde in the blue dress."

Luke scowled. "This is about Eva?"

"This is about wanting to prevent you from making the same mistakes that I made," Bailey told him.

"You really believe marrying Emily was a mistake?"

"I do," his brother said, and immediately grimaced. "And those are the words I never should have said the first time."

"When you left for New Mexico, you seemed so certain that it was what you wanted," Luke noted, troubled by the obvious disillusionment and bitterness in his brother's tone.

"If I've learned nothing else over the years, I've learned that I'm not certain about anything. Losing Mom and Dad, then being turned out by the grandparents, well, that kind of rejection can't help but screw up your mind and heart."

"You're right," Luke acknowledged. "But I believe that sometimes, if a man is very lucky, he might meet a woman who can help unscrew his mind and heart."

"And you think your blonde is that woman?" Bailey asked skeptically.

"Eva," he said again. "And yeah, I think she might be."

"How long have you known her?"

"A few weeks."

His brother's brows lifted. "You've known her a few weeks and you think she's the woman to fix everything that's broken inside you?"

"She's already made a start," he said.

"Or maybe you're looking for an excuse to stay in Rust Creek Falls and you're letting her be it."

Luke scowled. "That's not true. I have no intention of staying." Except that wasn't true, either. Not anymore.

"I know what it's like to feel alone, to miss family," Bailey told him. "Why do you think I finally went back to Wyoming?"

"You went back to Wyoming?"

His brother nodded. "I arrived early last week, but it

took me several days to track you down at Leaning Pines. It was your foreman who told me that you were in Rust Creek Falls for your brother's wedding. Of course, he didn't specify which brother, but my curiosity was piqued enough to follow your trail. I didn't expect to walk into a family reunion."

"An incomplete family reunion," Luke clarified.

"Yeah," Bailey acknowledged. "I guess no one knows where Liza is?"

"Bella's husband has been looking, but so far, no luck."

"That was a kicker, too," Bailey said. "Finding out that she was married—and to some rich guy from Oklahoma to boot."

"Hudson's a good guy," Luke told him.

"He seems to dote on our sister, that's for sure," Bailey agreed. "Of course, they haven't been married very long, either, have they? They're still in the honeymoon phase." He drained the last of his beer and held up the empty glass. "I'm going for a refill. Do you want anything?"

Luke shook his head. "No, thanks, I'm good."

But he wasn't.

His brother's words had put a damper on not just the evening but his whole outlook for the future, too.

He'd meant what he'd said to Eva. He'd never believed in the power of love, until he saw how it had changed his siblings. And while he couldn't deny that he had deep feelings for Eva, now he had to wonder if those feelings were deep enough.

Was he capable of loving her the way she deserved to be loved? Or was Bailey right? Had the death of his parents and subsequent rejection by his grandparents left him emotionally stunted?

* * *

Having finished her punch, Eva set the empty glass aside and walked over to where Luke was standing.

"Hey, cowboy." She nudged him playfully with her shoulder. "You promised me a dance."

His lips curved, but she noticed that the smile didn't reach his eyes.

"It's been a long time since I've danced," he warned. "And I can't promise I won't tread on those pretty shoes you're wearing."

"I'll take my chances," she assured him.

"In that case—" he offered his hand "—never let it be said that I'm not a man of my word."

He led her to the dance floor and turned her in his arms.

"Speaking of words," she said as they moved in rhythm with the music. "You started to say something earlier, before your brother interrupted us."

"Did I?" he hedged.

"Mmm-hmm," she confirmed. "Something about how your life has changed since you came home to Rust Creek Falls."

"It's been great to reconnect with my family," he said. "But Rust Creek Falls isn't my home. Not anymore."

"That's all you meant?" she asked, unable to hide the disappointment evident in her tone.

"That's why I came back," he reminded her.

"I know, but I thought—I hoped," she admitted, "you might find some other reasons to stay."

He looked away. "You know I can't."

But she didn't know any such thing. What she suspected was that Bailey had said something to cause

Luke's sudden withdrawal, because even while she was dancing with him, she could feel him pulling away.

"Do you really want to spend the rest of your life working as a ranch hand for somebody else?" she asked in a desperate attempt to open a dialogue with him.

"What other choice do I have?"

She lifted her hand from his shoulder and gestured to their surroundings. "You could put your time and energy into this place. Make Sunshine Farm a working ranch again."

She saw it then—a flicker of yearning in his eyes, there for only a second before it was shuttered away.

He shook his head. "That would be a lot more responsibility than I want to take on."

"Really?" she challenged.

"All I want is a paycheck, a six-pack and a willing woman at the end of the week."

The music continued to play but her feet stopped moving. "Is that all I was to you, Luke? A willing woman?"

He had the grace to look chagrined. "We had some good times together, Eva, but we both knew our relationship wasn't going to last."

In the past, whenever she'd been told the same or similar words, she'd quietly turned away rather than admit her heart was breaking. This time she lifted her chin and looked him straight in the eye.

"I disagree," she said. "I think that we had something pretty special together, but for some reason, you'd rather throw it away than give it a chance."

Then she turned away.

But she'd only taken a few steps when she pivoted on her heel to face him again. "As much as I'd like to storm out of here and leave you to contemplate my parting words, I need a ride home."

Under other circumstances, Eva's furious indignation might have made him smile, but Luke found it was impossible to smile while his heart was quietly bleeding. So he only reached into his pocket for his keys and said, "I'll take you."

"Thank you."

The cool primness of her tone didn't quite mask the hurt he'd caused, and he had to bite down on his tongue to prevent himself from offering excuses and explanations that wouldn't change anything in the end.

The ground outside was icy, and he automatically took her arm to help her navigate the treacherous terrain. She might have preferred to avoid his touch, but she was also practical enough to endure his assistance rather than end up on her butt.

She was quiet for the first several minutes of the drive back to her parents' house, and he wondered if she'd decided to never speak to him again. But then she broke the silence to ask, "What did he say to you?"

"Who?"

"Bailey," she said, somehow zeroing in on the topic that preoccupied his own mind.

He didn't deny that they'd talked—or that their conversation had changed the course of the evening for him. "He reminded me of some difficult truths I'd forgotten."

"What kind of truths?" she pressed.

He kept his gaze fixed on the road, not daring to look at her as he responded. "That the Stocktons are damaged."

"I don't believe it," she told him.

He pulled up in front of her parents' house, unable to squeeze into the driveway behind the two minivans that hadn't been there earlier—proof that her sisters and their families had arrived for the holiday.

He shifted into Park and turned off the ignition before he turned to face her. "I can't give you what you want, Eva. I don't have it within me."

"You can and you do," she insisted. "You're just afraid to admit your feelings."

"Feelings don't change anything. I told you in the beginning that I didn't want to get involved and I meant it."

"I love you, Luke."

He flinched as if she'd struck him. "Don't say that."

"Whether I speak the words or not, you know the feelings are true," she said. "You know how I feel about you."

He did. He'd told himself that her feelings were her own, that he wasn't responsible for her heart, but none of that helped him feel any better now.

"It's also true that I sometimes give my heart too easily," she told him. "I tried to hold back this time. I didn't want to fall in love with you, but I couldn't help myself. And I think you have some strong feelings for me, too."

She paused, as if giving him a chance to confirm or deny it. He didn't dare confirm it, and he couldn't honestly deny it, so he said nothing.

"But I'm not going to beg for scraps of affection," she continued when he remained silent. "Either you want to be with me or you don't. That's your choice to make and I'll accept whatever it is, but I'm going to suggest that you take some time to think about what you really want."

"Time isn't going to change anything," he said.

"Maybe not," she acknowledged, reaching for the handle of the door. "But I'm giving you a week anyway."

He hurried around to help her out of the vehicle. "Why a week?" he asked, curious about the arbitrary deadline she'd established even if it wouldn't change anything.

"Because there's a big party at Maverick Manor on New Year's Eve. If you decide that you feel the same way I do, you can meet me there. If you don't show up, I'll know that you don't, and I won't contact you again."

Then she slid her key into the lock of the front door.

"Eva."

She hesitated, for just a fraction of a second, before turning back.

But he didn't know what else to say. He only knew that he didn't want to leave her like this, with so much unspoken between them. Or maybe the problem was that too much had been spoken.

"Merry Christmas, Luke."

He dipped his head to touch his lips to her forehead. "Merry Christmas, Eva."

As Eva closed the door at her back, the click of the latch sounded loud in the quiet of the night. And final, like an exclamation mark at the end of a sentence—or the end of a relationship.

She felt the sting of tears behind her eyes, and stubbornly held them in check. She'd told Luke that she wasn't going to shed any tears over him and she meant it. The click of the latch notwithstanding, nothing was truly final yet. She'd given him a week to come to his senses and she had to trust that he would do so. If not, she would have plenty of time for tears in the New Year.

The house was dark and quiet, confirming that everyone had turned in early in anticipation of being awakened by the kids at the crack of dawn. But Eva knew that she was too unsettled to sleep right now, so she decided to make herself a cup of tea before heading up to bed.

Delphine wandered into the kitchen as Eva was pouring boiling water into a mug. Without needing to ask, she reached into the cupboard for a second mug, popped another tea bag into it and added water.

"Thanks," Del said, stifling a yawn as she accepted the mug her sister passed to her.

"I thought everyone was asleep already."

"I tried to wait up for you, but I snuggled with Freddy to help him settle down and fell asleep beside him."

"He's excited about Christmas," Eva guessed.

"They all are," her sister confirmed. "How was the wedding?"

She forced herself to push aside the painful memories of everything that had happened after and focus on the simple beauty of the ceremony. And remembering, she sighed wistfully. "It was beautiful."

"So why do you look so unhappy?"

"Because I did it again," she admitted.

"What did you do?"

"I fell in love with a man who doesn't love me back."

"The long-lost cowboy who recently returned to Rust Creek Falls?" Del guessed.

"Luke Stockton," Eva confirmed.

"The guy you went to the wedding with tonight?"

She nodded.

"How do you know he doesn't love you back?"

"Because he keeps reminding me of his plans to go back to Wyoming in the New Year."

"And you keep refusing to listen."

She sighed. "I was sure that when he had a chance

to see how good we were together, he would change his mind."

Del sighed. "Honey, you should know by now that it's a mistake to go into a relationship thinking you can change a man."

"I don't want to change *him*," she denied. "I just want him to change his geographical location."

"Asking a man to uproot himself from his job and his home and move eight hundred miles away is a big deal," her sister pointed out.

"I didn't ask him to move," she denied.

"But you want him to."

"I want it to be what he wants." She felt the sting of tears in her eyes. "*I* want to be what he wants."

Del reached across the table to squeeze her hand. "If you're not, then he's an idiot."

Eva managed a smile, but as she sipped her tea, she wondered why she always seemed to fall for the idiots.

Chapter Fifteen

In the usual chaos of Christmas morning, there was no time for self-indulgence or self-pity. After the mountain of presents had been opened and the debris cleared away, there were games to play and cars to race and LEGO cities to build. Through the course of the day, Eva barely had time to catch her breath much less feel sorry for herself. But through it all, she did realize something important.

She realized that, even if Luke didn't show up at Maverick Manor on New Year's Eve, even if she didn't yet have a partner to share her life, she was lucky to be surrounded by the love and support of her family.

And that, she knew, was a priceless gift—and one that Luke hadn't experienced in the past twelve years.

But this year would be different for him, because this year, he was with his family. She hoped he was having a good time with his siblings and their spouses and children. And she hoped that when he handed out the gifts they'd shopped for and wrapped together, he would think of her—for just a moment.

* * *

Luke was glad he'd decided to stay, not just for Danny and Annie's wedding but to celebrate Christmas with his siblings.

Because for the first time in a lot of years, it *was* a celebration.

Dana had to leave early in the morning to head back to Oregon because she had holiday traditions with her adoptive parents that she wanted to uphold, but she stayed long enough to have breakfast with Bella, Hudson, Luke and Bailey—who had spent the night in another one of the guest bedrooms. Jamie and Fallon showed up with Henry, Jared and Katie just as Dana was leaving, contributing to an even longer and more emotional goodbye scene. Then the rest of the family adjourned to the family room to open the presents that were under the tree.

He was grateful to Eva for her assistance with his shopping—and wrapping. Thinking back to that day, he couldn't help but remember the sparkle in her eyes, the warmth of her smile…and the expression of bliss on her face when their bodies joined together on the floor beneath this very Christmas tree.

Excusing himself from the gathering, he retreated to the kitchen to pour another cup of coffee. And steal another piece of the coffee cake that Bella had put out for breakfast and that he knew she'd picked up from Daisy's.

He was licking the crumbs off his fingers when his sister came in to refill her mug.

"Busted," she told him, softening the admonition with a smile.

He just shrugged. "What can I say? It's addictive."

"The cake or the baker?" she teased.

Instead of answering, he lifted his mug to his lips and sipped.

"You know, no one's going to mind if you want to slip away for a few hours," Bella told him.

"Why would I want to do that?"

She shook her head. "If I have to tell you, then you're not nearly as smart as I always thought you were."

"If you'd been in the truck when I took Eva home last night, you'd know that I'm an idiot."

"Were you a forgivable or unforgivable idiot?"

If you decide that you feel the same way I do, you can meet me there. If you don't show up, I'll know that you don't, and I won't contact you again.

He pushed the echo of Eva's words out of his mind. "It doesn't matter," he said. "Because I'm going back to Wyoming next week."

The teasing light in his sister's eyes immediately dimmed. "You're really leaving?"

"Isn't that what I've been saying all along?"

"It is," she admitted. "But I really thought you'd change your mind and decide to stay."

"I can't."

"You can," she insisted. "But you're stubborn and thick-headed and you're still punishing yourself for what happened to Mom and Dad. And, as a result, you're punishing the rest of us, too."

"You don't need me here, Bella."

She lifted her chin. "You're right. I don't need you in my life. I survived without you for almost twelve years and, if you leave, I'll continue to do so. But it's not what I want. I want you in my life."

"I'm not dropping off the face of the earth—I'm only going to Wyoming," he told her.

"What's so great about Wyoming?" Bella grumbled.

"It's where I live and work," he reminded her.

"You live in an apartment over a hardware store and you work on someone else's ranch."

He nodded his head in acknowledgment of those facts.

"If you stayed, you could live and work at Sunshine Farm."

"Bella—"

"I'm just putting it out there," she said. "Hudson told me not to pressure you, that you have to make your own choices about what's right for you. But I want to ensure you know what all your options are before you make that decision."

He slid an arm around her shoulders and drew her close. "The one thing I do know is that I'm going to miss my pain-in-the-butt sister when I'm gone."

She sniffled a little as she buried her face in his shirt. "I'll miss you, too, you big idiot."

While Eva and the other women were busy in the kitchen, preparing the big meal, the kids went out to play in the snow and the men were sent to supervise. A few minutes later, her brother-in-law Harrison came to the door asking for an extra hat and a scarf for the snowman they were building.

While Grandma went to the closet to see what she could find, Calla peeled potatoes, Del stirred her cranberry sauce and Eva worked on the relish trays for the table.

Marion came back with a hat and scarf and a square box wrapped in snowman paper with a big red bow on the top.

"I can't believe I forgot about this," she said, setting the box on the table beside Eva.

"What is it?" Calla asked.

"A present for Eva."

"For me?" she said, surprised.

Her mom nodded. "Luke dropped it off a few days ago and asked me to hide it until Christmas."

"It's from Luke?"

Marion nodded again.

"Well, go on," Del urged. "Open it."

She did so, tearing the paper at the end, then sliding the box out of the wrap.

"It's a cake stand," Calla said, clearly unimpressed.

Eva shook her head. "It's not a cake stand—it's a tilting turntable. You put the cake on top of it, then adjust the angle to make decorating easier."

"So…a cake stand," Calla said again.

But it was so much more than that to Eva. It was an extravagance that she hadn't been able to justify for herself, even when she'd noticed it was on sale the day she was shopping with Luke. And maybe she'd paused for a moment in front of it, but she'd never actually mentioned that she wanted one—and he hadn't asked.

But he'd clearly been paying attention.

And then he'd gone back to get it for her. But…why? Why would he do something so unexpectedly kind and thoughtful and then dump her a few days later?

"Well, that's…handy," her mother decided.

Eva laughed at the bafflement in her mother's tone. Maybe it wasn't flashy or extravagant, but that cake decorating tool proved that Luke knew her better than most of the other men she'd dated—and even most of her family.

While Marion took the snowman accessories to the

door and Calla resumed her peeling, Del leaned close and whispered in Eva's ear, "I'm starting to think that maybe he's not such an idiot, after all."

He was an idiot to even be considering this.

Luke had told Eva that he was going back to Wyoming and that was exactly what he should do.

Instead, he was putting a noose around his neck— literally.

"You'd be much more handsome if you'd stop scowling."

He glanced at his sister's reflection behind his own in the mirror. "I hate wearing a tie."

"You certainly don't know how to tie one," Bella noted.

"This was a bad idea anyway," he said, tugging at the knot.

"No, it's a good idea," she said. "It's just the execution that needs some work."

"I'm not just talking about the tie."

"Neither am I." She brushed his hands aside and pulled the ends, adjusting the length before she began making the knot.

He watched, fascinated, as she quickly and expertly completed the task that he'd struggled with unsuccessfully. "Where did you learn how to do that?"

"Watching Hudson," she admitted.

"He wears one of these every day, doesn't he?"

"Mmm-hmm," she agreed.

"Why?" he wondered.

"I'm not sure, but he looks good in a tie. And without a tie. And without—"

"TMI, little sister," he interjected.

She laughed softly. "And when a man who doesn't usually wear a tie puts one on for a woman, it tells her that she matters."

"Does it?" he asked dubiously.

"Of course, if you had a diamond ring in the pocket of that jacket, it would say the same thing much more effectively."

"If I had a diamond ring in my pocket, don't you think I should show it to Eva before I showed it to you?"

"I'm not asking to *see* it, I'm just asking if you *have* it," Bella pressed.

"Thanks for your help with the tie."

"Anytime." She tugged on the accessory in question. "And I mean that, Luke. I'm happy to help you with anything, anytime. Of course, it would be easier to lend a helping hand if you were living in Rust Creek Falls."

"You never quit, do you?"

"Perseverance is one of my many charms."

"Is that what your husband tells you?"

She grinned. "All the time."

"He's a smart man."

"Smart enough to put a ring on my finger," Bella agreed.

He took his sister by the shoulders and turned her gently toward the door. "Go find that smart husband of yours so that you can go out and celebrate the New Year together."

As she did so, he scooped his keys off the dresser and headed out to his truck. But the closer he got to his destination, the more questions and doubts that assailed him.

Was he doing the right thing?

He eased up on the gas as he approached the entrance

to Maverick Manor, but instead of turning in to the drive, he kept going.

Because there was still a part of him that believed Eva would be better off if he returned to Cheyenne. Then she would be free to fall in love with a man who wasn't burdened with the kind of baggage that weighed him down. And there was no doubt in his mind that Eva deserved better than him.

But in the few weeks that he'd known her, she'd already helped to lighten the load he carried. Of course, talking to his siblings had helped, too. Their support and acceptance had given him hope that he could finally move forward with his life, but it was Eva who had given him hope that he didn't have to move forward alone.

With her sweetness and kindness and patience, she had shown him that he wasn't only worthy of being loved, but that he was capable of loving in return. Because he knew now that he did love her—and he didn't ever want to leave her.

Unfortunately he came to that realization about an hour after he'd driven past Maverick Manor, which meant that it would be another hour before he could get back. And it was almost eleven o'clock already.

He checked his mirrors to confirm that there were no other vehicles around, then made a U-turn in the middle of the road and stepped on the accelerator.

Eva had practically floated through the day, buoyed by foolish hope that she'd walk into Maverick Manor and find Luke waiting for her. But he wasn't there.

Of course, she hadn't given him a specific time and, in retrospect, she could acknowledge that "New Year's Eve" was a little vague. Just because he wasn't there promptly at eight o'clock didn't mean he wasn't going to show up.

But eight o'clock had become nine o'clock, which was when Travis and Brenna were scheduled to renew their vows in front of their families and friends. As Eva watched them promise to love, honor and cherish one another, she couldn't help but wonder if she would ever find a man to look at her the way Travis looked at Brenna. For a very short while, she'd let herself believe that Luke Stockton might be that man, but his absence from the festivities tonight forced her to accept that she'd been wrong.

When the groom was instructed to kiss his bride, he did so with lavish enthusiasm and Eva lifted a tissue to dab at the moisture on her lower lashes. More than a few of the female guests were wiping their eyes, and she trusted that anyone who saw her tears would assume they were a response to the emotional ceremony. Only she knew the truth—that at least a few of those tears were for herself, for the weary heart that had been rejected yet again.

As she looked around the room, hoping for a quiet corner to escape to for a minute, she couldn't help but take note of all the happy couples and families in attendance. Newlyweds Autry Jones and Marissa Fuller were there with her daughters Abby, Kiera and Kaylee, the girls all sporting festive berets from their recent trip to Paris; and Abby's BFF, Janie Lattimore, who was staying with her dad, Hank, while her mom, Annie, was off on her honeymoon with her other dad, Danny, in celebration of their Christmas Eve wedding. Lydia Grant was cozied up in the corner with Zach Dalton, and Eva had heard rumors that a springtime wedding was being planned for the recently engaged couple. Hadley Strickland was wearing a ring on the third finger of her left hand now, too, and was in attendance with her doting fiancé Eli Dalton. Because everyone in town was pairing up and falling in love.

Everyone except Eva.

Well, she'd done the falling in love part.

Unfortunately, Luke hadn't fallen in love, too.

And now it was after eleven o'clock and, as each minute passed, she became more and more certain that he wasn't going to show up. How could she have misread the situation so badly? Was she so desperate for love that she only saw what she wanted to see?

She didn't believe it. The way Luke had looked at her, kissed her, touched her, she'd been certain that he had deep feelings for her.

But tonight was New Year's Eve and he wasn't anywhere around, forcing Eva to acknowledge the possibility that she might never see him again.

She glanced at the slender gold watch on her wrist—a gift from her parents when she graduated high school—and felt her heart sink a little deeper. It was almost eleven thirty now. She looked around the room again. There were so many people packed into the ballroom that she wasn't sure she would be able to pick him out of the crowd if he was there. But she felt confident that she would know it in her heart—and right now, her heart was empty.

"Can I have this dance?"

The voice was familiar, albeit not the voice she longed to hear. But she forced a smile and turned to Bobby Ray Ellis. She didn't want to dance with anyone but Luke, but she also didn't want to look like a pathetic wallflower. It was New Year's Eve and this was a party, so she would dance with anyone who asked and pretend that her heart wasn't shattered into a million pieces.

It was almost midnight by the time Luke pulled into the very full parking lot of Maverick Manor. He scanned for an empty space, certain that everyone in Rust Creek Falls had turned out for the New Year's Eve party. Or maybe they were here to watch the reality TV newly-weds renew their vows. Either way, the prospect of such a crowd had a bead of sweat sliding down his back.

He preferred intimate gatherings to boisterous parties, and there weren't a lot of women that he would venture near a fancy shindig like this for. In fact, he couldn't imagine doing it for anyone but Eva. Because he loved her.

He wasn't sure that he was worthy of her heart, but he wasn't foolish enough to let a woman like her slip through his fingers. Yeah, he had scars, and they went pretty deep. But Eva had seen them all and she loved him anyway.

The doors of the hotel opened up, spilling out light and music and a familiar figure in a black dress. A very little black dress. His mouth went dry and his heart, already racing, started to pound even harder and faster.

But Eva didn't see him. Nor did she seem to be looking for him. Instead, she ducked behind a support column, as if she wanted to be alone, and dropped her chin to her chest.

He'd started eagerly toward the entrance as soon as he saw her, but now his steps faltered.

Was she…crying?

Of course she was, and even an idiot could figure out why. Because she'd asked him to meet her tonight, to prove that he cared about her, and she thought he was a no-show.

The absolute last thing he'd ever want to do was hurt her, but the streaks of moisture on her cheeks confirmed the painful truth. The tears were his fault.

But he could fix this—he *would* fix this. And he would spend the rest of his life making it up to her, if she would let him.

"Eva?"

Her head came up fast and her eyes, swimming with tears, met his for only a brief moment before they slid away again.

"What—" the word sounded a little hoarse, and she paused to clear her throat before continuing "—what are you doing here?"

"Isn't this where you told me to be?" He took another step closer. His gaze roamed over her hungrily, taking in every detail from the spiraling curls piled on her head to the strapless figure-hugging dress that ended several inches above her knees and the ice-pick heels on her feet. "You look…wow."

And a little cold, he realized, noting the goose bumps on her arms. He unbuttoned his jacket and draped it over her shoulders.

"Thanks," she said, then gave him a casual once-over and offered a small smile. "You clean up pretty good yourself, cowboy."

"I hate wearing a tie," he admitted.

"Why did you?"

"Because—" he reached for her hands and linked their fingers together "—according to my sister, when a man who doesn't usually wear a tie puts one on for a woman, it tells her that she matters."

"Words could probably accomplish the same thing."

"I'm not always good with words," he confided. "But I'm here—and wearing a tie—because you matter."

She dropped her gaze to their joined hands. "I thought you weren't going to show up," she admitted.

"I'm sorry I'm late," he said.

"You're here," she said, and offered a tremulous smile. "That's the important thing."

"Do you remember telling me that my story wasn't over? That I could write a happy ending if I wanted it?"

She nodded.

"I want that happy ending—with you." He dropped his hands so that he could draw her into his embrace. "I love you, Eva."

"I love you, too," she said.

Inside the crowd began the countdown to midnight.

"Ten..."

"I didn't intend to cut it this close," he told her.

"...nine..."

"We still have nine seconds."

"...eight..."

"Eight," she amended.

"I want to kiss you at midnight, so I'll have to talk fast."

"...seven..."

"Or we could skip the talking and move—"

"...six..."

"—right to the kissing."

"...five..."

He reached for the box in his pocket—only to remember that she was now wearing his jacket. He patted his hands down her sides, searching.

"Or the awkward, fumbling foreplay," she teased.

"...four..."

He found the box and dropped to a knee in front of her. "Will you marry me, Eva?"

Her eyes went wide and she lifted a hand to press it to her heart. "Ohmygod—I feel like I'm dreaming."

"...three..."

"You're not dreaming," he assured her. "You're also not answering my question."

"...two..."

"You really want to marry me?"

"...one..."

"More than anything else in the world."

"Then yes," she said quickly. "My answer is yes."

He slid the ring on her finger.

"Happy New Year!"

He smiled. "Happy New Year, Eva."

"Happy New Year, Luke."

Then, finally, he was kissing her.

And Eva forgot that she was standing outside at midnight on New Year's Eve in twenty-degree weather because being in Luke's arms warmed everything inside her.

While he continued to kiss her, she became aware of something that sounded like...clapping?

Then someone said, "Now that gives a whole new meaning to the expression 'ring in the New Year.'"

Luke reluctantly eased his mouth from hers, but he kept his arms around her, holding her close. "While your enthusiasm is appreciated," he said dryly, "you're interrupting a private moment here."

"I didn't mean to intrude," the stranger said. "But that really was perfect. In fact, I don't think my producer could have scripted it any better."

"Producer?" Eva echoed warily, noting the camera propped casually on his shoulder.

"Of *The Great Roundup*. That's why I was here—to film Travis and Brenna's renewal of vows," the man explained. "I was on my way out when I caught a glimpse of something from the corner of my eye and started the camera rolling. I got the whole proposal—and that really hot kiss."

Luke didn't look happy to hear his admission. "You recorded us—without our knowledge or consent?"

"The candid stuff is always the best," the cameraman said. "Do you guys think you'd be interested in taking part in the show next season?"

Eva had enjoyed watching Travis and Brenna compete for the big prize—and Luke hadn't grumbled too much about it—but she didn't think either of them wanted that kind of fame or fortune. She looked at him now, and they both shook their heads.

The man pressed a card into Luke's hand. "In case you change your mind."

Then, finally, he took his camera and walked away.

"You're not going to change your mind, are you?" Luke asked.

"No," she said. "I don't want to be famous. I just want to be with you."

"Good." He brushed a sweet kiss on her lips. "Because that's everything I want, too."

Epilogue

"Are you sure you want to do this?" Eva asked, seeking reassurance before she slid the scraper under the seam of the wallpaper.

"I'm sure this paper is hideous," Luke told her. "Which means that it has to go."

She looked at the printed ivy that seemed to crawl up the walls, and though it wasn't anything she ever would have chosen, she didn't think it was ugly so much as dated. Which made sense, considering that his parents had papered the kitchen walls some twenty years earlier.

Even when Luke had decided that he wanted to stay in Rust Creek Falls with Eva, he'd balked at the idea of moving back to his childhood home. But over time she'd managed—with the encouragement and support of his siblings—to counter his objections.

They hadn't decided what they were going to do with the land, because they were still looking for Liza so that all of the siblings would have input into that decision, and Hudson's PI hadn't had much luck in tracking her down. But David Bradford had done some digging locally and discovered that Matthew Baldwin was the one who had paid the taxes on Sunshine Farm. The *why* was still unknown and the old man had rejected all efforts by his grandchildren to find out, but Eva was confident the truth would be revealed in short order.

For now, Luke and Eva were working toward making the house livable again, one room at a time. They'd tackled the master bedroom first, for obvious reasons; then Luke had wanted to redo the kitchen—for Eva.

"I was trying to decide what room to do after we're finished with the kitchen," Luke said as he scraped the paper on the wall next to where Eva was working.

"We've just started with the kitchen," she reminded him.

"I know," he admitted. "But when it's done, maybe we could do the bedroom across the hall from ours."

"Don't you think it makes more sense to focus on the main floor first?" she said.

"We could do what makes sense—" he said, holding his palms up as if they were scales and he was weighing the options "—or we could make a baby."

The scraper slipped from Eva's hand and clattered to the floor. She left it where it fell and turned to face him. "You want to have a baby?"

"Well, not before we're married," he said. "But yeah, in the not-too-distant future. As long as it's what you want, too."

"Yeah, it's definitely what I want, too."

Then she lifted her arms to link them behind his head and drew his mouth down to hers.

"In fact," she said, whispering the words against his lips, "I think we should go upstairs now and check out the bedroom you were talking about."

"You just want to get me upstairs so that you can seduce me."

"You don't know me as well as you think you do," she said, shaking her head in mock disapproval as she reached for the buckle of his belt. "Or you'd realize that I can seduce you anywhere."

"You've got me there," he admitted. "In fact, you've got me anywhere you want me."

She kissed him again. "Which is only one of the many reasons I love you."

"I love you, too," he said, and proceeded to show her how very much.

* * * * *

*Can't get enough of those Mavericks?
Don't miss our bonus Montana Mavericks
summer special.*

*Vivienne Shuster is an expert wedding planner, but her
own love life is a disaster—and now she needs a fiancé
to impress her boss! Cole Dalton thinks
weddings are for the birds. Can he cowboy up and help
Viv—without falling for the
Rust Creek Falls marriage magic?*

*Look for
THE MAVERICK'S BRIDAL BARGAIN
by
Christy Jeffries*

*Available June 2017,
wherever Harlequin books and ebooks are sold.*

And catch up with the rest of the
MONTANA MAVERICKS:
THE GREAT FAMILY ROUNDUP

Look for:
THE MAVERICK FAKES A BRIDE
by New York Times *Bestselling Author*
Christine Rimmer

MOMMY AND THE MAVERICK by Meg Maxwell

THE MAVERICK'S BRIDE-TO-ORDER
by USA TODAY *Bestselling Author Stella Bagwell*

THE MAVERICK'S RETURN
by USA TODAY *Bestselling Author Marie Ferrarella*

THE MAVERICK'S SNOWBOUND CHRISTMAS
by USA TODAY *Bestselling Author Karen Rose Smith*

THE MAVERICK'S MIDNIGHT PROPOSAL
by Brenda Harlen

COMING NEXT MONTH FROM

HARLEQUIN®

SPECIAL EDITION

Available December 19, 2017

#2593 HER SOLDIER OF FORTUNE
The Fortunes of Texas: The Rulebreakers • by Michelle Major
When Nathan Fortune returned home, he vowed to put the past behind him. But when Bianca, his best friend's little sister, shows up with her son, Nate finds that the past won't stay buried...and it threatens to snuff out the future Nate and Bianca now hope to build with each other.

#2594 THE ARIZONA LAWMAN
Men of the West • by Stella Bagwell
Tessa Parker goes to Arizona to investigate her unexpected inheritance and gets more than a ranch. There's a sexy deputy next door and perhaps this orphan may finally find a family on the horizon.

#2595 JUST WHAT THE COWBOY NEEDED
The Bachelors of Blackwater Lake • by Teresa Southwick
Logan Hunt needs a nanny. What he gets is pretty kindergarten teacher Grace Flynn, whose desire for roots and a family flies right in the face of Logan's determination to remain a bachelor. Can Logan overcome his fears of becoming his father in time to convince Grace that she's exactly what he wants?

#2596 CLAIMING THE CAPTAIN'S BABY
American Heroes • by Rochelle Alers
Former army captain and current billionaire Giles Wainwright is shocked to learn he has a daughter and even more shocked at how attracted he is to her adoptive mother, Mya Lawson. But Mya doesn't trust Giles's motives when it comes to her heart and he will have to work harder than ever if he wants to claim Mya's love.

#2597 THE RANCHER AND THE CITY GIRL
Sweet Briar Sweethearts • by Kathy Douglass
Running for her life, Camille Parker heads to her sworn enemy, Jericho Jones, for protection. She may be safe from those who wish her harm, but as they both come to see their past presumptions proven incorrect, Camille's heart is more at risk than ever.

#2598 BAYSIDE'S MOST UNEXPECTED BRIDE
Saved by the Blog • by Kerri Carpenter
Riley Hudson is falling for her best friend and boss, Sawyer Wallace, the only person who knows she is the ubiquitous Bayside Blogger. Awkward as that could be, though, they both have bigger problems in the form of blackmail and threats to close down the newspaper they both work for! Will Sawyer see past that long enough to make Riley Bayside's most unexpected bride?

YOU CAN FIND MORE INFORMATION ON UPCOMING HARLEQUIN® TITLES, FREE EXCERPTS AND MORE AT WWW.HARLEQUIN.COM.

HSECNM1217

Get 2 Free Books,
Plus 2 Free Gifts—
just for trying the
Reader Service!

♦ HARLEQUIN®
SPECIAL EDITION

"He's an idiot," Nate offered automatically.

One side of her mouth kicked up. "You sound like Eddie. He never liked Brett, even when we were first dating. He said he wasn't good enough for me."

"Obviously that's true." Nate took a step closer but stopped himself before he reached for her. Bianca didn't belong to him, and he had no claim on her. But one morning with EJ and he already felt a connection to the boy. A connection he also wanted to explore with the beautiful woman in front of him. "Any man who would walk away from you needs to have his—" He paused, feeling the unfamiliar sensation of color rising to his face. His mother had certainly raised him better than to swear in front of a lady, yet the thought of Bianca being hurt by her ex made his blood boil. "He needs a swift kick in the pants."

"Agreed," she said with a bright smile. A smile that

made him weak in the knees. He wanted to give her a reason to smile like that every day. "I'm better off without him, but it still makes me sad for EJ. I do my best, but it's hard with only the two of us. There are so many things we've had to sacrifice." She wrapped her arms around her waist and turned to gaze out of the barn, as if she couldn't bear to make eye contact with Nate any longer. "Sometimes I wish I could give him more."

"You're enough," he said, reaching out a hand to brush away the lone tear that tracked down her cheek. "Don't doubt for one second that you're enough."

As he'd imagined, her skin felt like velvet under his callused fingertip. Her eyes drifted shut and she tipped up her face, as if she craved his touch as much as he wanted to give it to her.

He wanted more from this woman—this moment— than he'd dreamed possible. A loose strand of hair brushed the back of his hand, sending shivers across his skin.

She glanced at him from beneath her lashes, but there was no hesitation in her gaze. Her liquid brown eyes held only invitation, and his entire world narrowed to the thought of kissing Bianca.

"I finished with the hay, Mommy," EJ called from behind him.

Don't miss
HER SOLDIER OF FORTUNE by Michelle Major,
available January 2018 wherever
Harlequin® Special Edition books and ebooks are sold.

www.Harlequin.com

HSEEXP1217

LOVE
Harlequin
romance?

Join our Harlequin community to share your thoughts and connect with other romance readers!

Be the first to find out about promotions, news, and exclusive content!

Sign up for the Harlequin e-newsletter and download a free book from any series at

www.TryHarlequin.com

CONNECT WITH US AT:

Harlequin.com/Community

 Facebook.com/HarlequinBooks

Twitter.com/HarlequinBooks

Instagram.com/HarlequinBooks

Pinterest.com/HarlequinBooks

ReaderService.com

 HARLEQUIN®

**ROMANCE WHEN
YOU NEED IT**

HSOCIAL2017

THE WORLD IS BETTER WITH

Romance

Harlequin has everything from contemporary, passionate and heartwarming to suspenseful and inspirational stories.

Whatever your mood,
we have a romance just for you!